NIGHTMARE ALLEY PRESENTS

Night Terrors

Vol. 1

by

Professor Spooky

Edited by Amanda Faustina

Cover by designrans

Cover Image © Aditya Chinchure

Nightmare Alley Logo by Heino Brand

Back Cover Image © Estaban Lopez-Formaz

CONTENTS

INTRODUCTION

The tales of terror found inside this slim collection of short stories began with a fever dream, a compulsion to create, and a desire to throw off the yoke of editorial control and publisher interference. The collective of writers that came together to form the Nightmare Alley YouTube channel are all professional writers actively working in many mediums. The channel has not been around long, but their output has been horrifyingly prolific. They are true fans of the horror genre. And they are masters of it.

The five stories that you are about to devour have all been written since the launch of their YouTube channel in the summer of 2019. This is hopefully just a small taste of what's to come.

Special thanks go out to Brian "Barncat" Lee for narrating the stories that bring us all night terrors. Without Brian's voice or Roger Wright's expert recording equipment and post-production skills, these stories would not have found an audience. Additional thanks goes to New-York Times Best-Selling Author Micky Neilson for lending his time and talent to the collective and for Amanda Faustina for stepping out of the comment section and into her editorial capacity on this project. While Brian and Roger steer the audio side of things, Micky and Amanda ensure our print efforts maintain the high level of quality Nightmare Alley projects deserve. Combined, they are Nightmare Alley.

Professor Spooky,

Bellingham, WA

July 2020

Doom Bunny: Quarantine Knight

Doom Bunny *came into the world in the spring of 2020 during the COVID lockdown. Professor Spooky has long wanted to set a story in the town of Bellingham, WA. Weaving in his love for Lovecraftian lore throughout the Urban Legend of Doom Bunny seemed necessary. The empty streets and increasingly erratic behavior of the town's homeless demanded it. The Cycle of Azathoth goes on.*

"...one night a mighty gulf was bridged, and the dream-haunted skies swelled down to the lonely watcher's window to merge with the close air of his room and make him a part of their fabulous wonder."

–H.P. Lovecraft

Bellingham was getting really creepy under quarantine. The bay town was always a little weird, but something about the COVID quarantine took it to the next level. Shops and restaurants were closed. The streets were devoid of the usual college-aged dipshits and microbrew connoisseurs that usually plagued the streets nearly every night of the week. It was practically a ghost town during the day. But come night things were odd, like the matrix was broken odd.

I had been driving Uber for a couple years and had grown very educated in what people actually meant by "Bellingweird." It wasn't just the meth and fentanyl or the mentally ill homeless that lived on the outskirts of everyone's peripheral vision. It wasn't the cornrow-wearing stoner townies or the corner drunks panhandling in front of the Horse Shoe Cafe. I mean, yeah, it was those things, but there was something else. Like the homeless and beat cops were arming for a war that normal people had no idea was brewing. Anyone who paid attention long enough could tell the homeless weren't just harmless panhandlers down on their luck. Some of them anyway.

They weren't all merely bipolar junkies bumming bus fare by day and shooting up at night. Some of them—a growing number of them—were operating with intention and increasing urgency. That feeling didn't cease when the town went on lockdown. If anything, it seemed to elevate the foreboding feeling. The near-empty streets were thick with it. Static charged. I could feel the intensity grow. It was palpable. It felt, at the same time, like a physical weight thickening the air I was breathing. It felt like my nerves were slowly being pulled to an inevitable breaking point.

"Frayed" didn't even begin to describe how my nerves felt.

Every night I parked down by Holly and Railroad waiting for the Uber app to ping in my ear to alert me that I had a passenger to pick up. Usually it was just to take someone home after grocery shopping or to give some stoner a ride to and from a weed dispensary. Most people on the streets wore masks and kept their distance, but the homeless—or at least a subset of them—had begun wearing masks *months* before anyone ever heard of COVID-19. They had started arming themselves with staves and clubs about the same time. Maybe a little earlier. Some of them beat on impromptu drums. Garbage cans mostly. Somehow, they all drummed to the same beat. A primordial beat that didn't help my frayed nerves at all.

The world was going to hell, and I was sure I was losing my mind. I was barely making money to pay my bills before the pandemic. Once the lockdown hit, not only did the Uber customers drop way off but I was risking my life picking up total strangers—just so I could scrape up enough to pay a phone bill and put some gas in my shitty Toyota Sienna. Once I gassed up at the end of the night, I'd *maybe* grab a .99 cent can of chili from the local loser store known as the Gross Out. That's not the world I thought we were going to live in when I graduated school thirty years earlier and the Soviet Union was collapsing.

Yay for Super Capitalism.

Anyway...

The only people out at night under the quarantine were homeless people and rando townies who couldn't bother to wear their masks to the weed stores. Cops were sparse. Strange considering how much they overpopulated the streets when everything was normal. One night, things were really slow. I was sipping a Coke in my minivan, not giving a single shit that I was pre-diabetic, when I heard a rap on the passenger-side door. I'd have recognized that heavily-tattooed torso anywhere.

I didn't know the guy's name, but I had seen him a few summers earlier. The town had been a total smoke show that summer thanks to all the surrounding wildfires. I was parked back behind the abandoned Pacific Market trying not to get violently ill from the smoke I was ingesting when a fight broke out in a make-shift meth head camp. The meth must have been especially potent that summer. The homeless were in fine form all over town. Super aggressive and wild eyed. They were a bunch of yammering idiots who had no issue walking right out into traffic and mad dogging drivers who had the gall to break for them.

I called 911 to report the fight when shirtless guy strolled out of the smoke and up to the makeshift parking-lot camp. The only piece of clothing he wore was a pair of tattered, dark-denim jeans. His upper body was covered in symbols. I had no idea what the symbols meant, but they were not normal tattoos. More like evenly sized stamps riddling his torso, neck, and arms. The smoke was thick so I couldn't make out his face. He just came out of the nasty, caustic shit like a shirtless Batman and pulled the homeless dudes apart. One of them tried to go after him, but shirtless guy knocked him out with the hardest, most casual punch I've ever watched anyone throw. I couldn't hear anything inside my Sienna—except the sickly wet impact of that punch as it connected with the froggy guy's face. Shirtless guy gestured to the other homeless dude before he slipped back into the smog, walking in the general direction of Cornwall Street. Panic-eyed, the last homeless guy standing gathered up a few belongings and skittered away in a manner that only a meth head could skitter.

I waited for the cops to show. I left a statement with a surprisingly young and attractive policewoman named Officer Carter. She took my statement, warned me to stay away from shirtless guy, then moved to inspect the meth camp. She had asked me to describe the tattoos, but the guy had been too far away for me to really identify anything. The officer looked annoyed by that. Abnormally so. I had no idea what that was about and didn't care. I never wanted to see those intense green eyes again. I drove off as soon as she started heading to the camp in the general direction of the unconscious guy still laying in the parking lot. I mean, I had seen a couple tattoos that had seared into my mind, but I had no idea how to describe them.

I hadn't seen shirtless guy again until he knocked on my car door.

Not really wanting to do anything but drive off, I slipped my totally not N95 mask on and cracked the window. He wasn't bending down, so I had no idea what he looked like. All I could see were the strange symbols littering his body.

"Yeah?" I asked.

"I need a ride to the Coachman Inn," he said in a deep, muffled voice. Man, he freaked me out. He must have spotted the Uber decal I left sitting on my dashboard. I was too stubborn to stick it to the window like city ordinance required.

"Can you hail me on the app?"

"I don't use a phone," he said as matter-of-fact as if he said he doesn't have a VCR.

"Do you have cash?" I asked against my better judgment. I really needed some cash, but holy shit, did I not want to give this guy a ride.

"Yeah," he replied in that strange muffled voice.

I let out a deep breath of nervous air.

"Okay, hop in the back seat," I said, unlocking the door for him.

I started the engine and reflexively checked my mirror for oncoming traffic as I heard the side door slide open. I needn't have bothered. The streets were barren and oddly beautiful as twilight turned to night and the street lights lit up the wide strip of Holly for as far as the eye could see. As he slid the door shut, I took a hard look at him in the rear view mirror. I instantly regretted letting him into my shitty minivan. He was definitely the guy I saw a few summers earlier. Maybe he had a few more tattoos. Maybe he had packed on a few more pounds of muscle across his shoulders and chest. But the matte-black bunny helmet was new.

Yeah, bunny helmet. Let me try to capture the essence of this. This helmet was not one of those fun and sassy motorcycle helmets you can find on Amazon for your Asian girlfriend. This thing was industrial and hand crafted. It was a clumsy patchwork of welded together bits that were fabricated by someone who never took entry level metal working. It looked like it at one time had been an antique deep-sea diver's helmet by the way the neck of it came down over his shoulders and how big and thick the helmet was. The original viewports in the front and side had been cut away. In the front, large vertical slots had been cut out and fine mesh had been clumsily welded over them. The same mesh was used to cover the side viewports as well. No wonder his voice was so muted. There was no mouth hole. Just the vents were the viewports once were. What truly put it all over the top was the crudely fabricated bunny ears mounted onto the top of the helmet. Everything was sloppily spray painted in matte-black paint. It looked like white chalk had recently been used to draw in a cartoonish mouth with big chunky teeth, but had been smudged almost beyond recognition.

Shirtless guy was no craftsman. What he was was tall and massively muscled, so he had to slouch down low in the chair to clear the minivan ceiling. His head cocked at a comical angle so the bunny ears wouldn't bang on the roof of the vehicle.

I'm a thoughtful guy, so I opened the sunroof for him and told him he could drop the seat back if he wanted to.

"Thank you," he said, immediately adjusting the seat to angle his bunny ears out the sunroof while he fished in his front pocket.

He slid a battered ten-dollar bill into my hands. I tossed it into the glove box beside my Lysol spray for later deconning as I pulled out onto Holly and crossed a few lanes to make the next left turn. At the intersection, I could hear a primal beat being drummed out on what I imagined was an upside down bucket. It just kinda had that sound to it. The street was otherwise deserted, and I didn't feel like peering into the darkened stoops of shops to figure out which transient was killing time with that unnerving beat.

"We're going to the Coachman?" I reflexively asked, confirming the drop off. I was trying to shake off the sound of the drumming and focus on my passenger, but that beat had a way of getting into my head.

"Yeah," he replied. I couldn't be certain, but I felt as if he was studying my reflection in the rearview mirror. Like he was sizing me up. So there we were in my minivan. Him studying his masked Uber driver; me studying the tattooed shirtless guy in a giant bunny helmet. "Can I have you wait for me?" he continued. "I'll only be there for fifteen minutes. I need to be at Old School in an hour."

The tattoo parlor had only been a half block away from where I picked the guy up.

"Okay. That'll be another ten bucks. I'll need to get paid when we get to the Coachman."

He retrieved a couple crumpled fives and handed them to me. They went right where I put his other bill. I really wanted to grab a Lysol wipe but didn't want to offend the guy.

"You sure do have a lot of tattoos," I said, knowing how dumb it sounded before I even said it.

I could feel him staring at me like I was an asshole.

"Sorry, I'm sure you hear that a lot," I tried to recover. "I just think they're cool. What do they represent?"

The tension in the air eased. Without looking down, not that he would have been able to, he pointed to a fist-sized symbol over his heart.

"This is a ward. They're all wards. Or sigils. This one in particular enhances both my physical and magickal strength."

My interest genuinely perked. I was an old-school RPGer and avid horror-fiction fan. I knew what wards were. I kicked myself for not noticing the symbols for what they obviously were earlier.

"Like, magical wards?" I asked, scanning his torso in the mirror to see if I recognized any. Most were about the same fist-sized symbols. Nearly all of them were encircled. I saw a pentacle and several symbols that represented the fire element. I didn't know what all the permutations were or why some of them were in boxes instead of circles.

"Yeah, like magic," he said. "This one's an advanced protection ward," he continued, pointing to something that to me looked like a Celtic symbol. Kinda like a knot but also not like that. "This one allows me to heal faster when injured. This symbol makes me more emotionally stable and wards off insanity. I should probably get it touched up."

"Damn," I said, genuinely interested. I mean, the guy was clearly a nut and I was probably going to get murdered, but my curiosity got the better of me. "What's the one with the crossed out eye?" The eye looked a little like the one found on the dollar bill. But a bold "X" was inked over it.

"Invisibility ward. It helps keep me unseen from…from certain things and types of people," he answered. He obviously didn't want to talk about that.

"What's the X with the horizontal line through it?" I asked.

"Helps me lose weight," he said as I turned into one of the many crack hotels Bellingham had to offer. The ward must have worked. The guy didn't have a single ounce of fat on him. "Stay right and go around back," he continued.

I followed his instructions until he told me to stop at the very back of the motel. Perfect place for a tweaker to hole up.

He handed me another ten bucks as he stepped out of the vehicle.

"In case I take a little longer than expected. Please don't leave me stranded."

I nodded as I accepted his money.

"Hey, what's the symbol on the inside of your wrist?" I asked, not sure why it intrigued me so much. "Is it a fire symbol?"

He paused. Maybe he was impressed that I knew a tiny bit about magical wards. Maybe he was just annoyed that I was delaying him. I couldn't tell what he was thinking behind that enormous bunny helmet.

"Yeah, fire. But not just fire. It's also a Level 3 Child Protection ward."

"Really? That's really cool. Where did you get it? I kinda want one."

"Everyone should want one. But you have to earn it."

The side door slid shut with a bang before I had a chance to say anything else.

I started deconning my hands and steering wheel while he ascended a set of stairs. I watched him being let into room 218 as I slipped my earbuds in and flipped on an audiobook. I noted that he had a long, intricate tattoo that ran down his spine. I recognized it as a sigil representing the cosmos. I only learned it from some research I did when I used to dungeon master a group of role players a decade ago. I recalled something about lining the sigil up with one's chakras for a variety of spiritual benefits. What a weird dude. What an absolutely bizarre situation to find myself in.

The air felt electric. Everything felt strange and stretched to its breaking point. I had lost track of time. I was that deep in thought. I wasn't even sure what I was thinking about. Really, I was just mindlessly staring at the sick glow of a nearby street light as it flickered and threatened to burn out.

A loud banging on the driver-side door snapped me out of it. I flinched when I realized shirtless guy was staring in at me. No one wanted to wake up to find that creepy bunny helmet looming over them.

"It's time to go," he said. "We need to move quickly."

We were back on the road as fast as I could shake my funk.

"Are you okay?" he asked. He had been studying me from the back seat.

"Yeah, I'm fine," I replied. "Sorry, I'm a little out of it."

"You should get a ward to improve your energy and mental clarity."

I glanced at him in the rearview mirror, nodding my head. It wasn't a bad idea. I always wanted to dabble with some tattoos, but it would have to wait until I was making real money again.

"Old School, right?" I finally replied.

"Yeah. As fast as you can. I'm behind schedule."

"You got it," I said, absently, accelerating as much as I reasonably could on an empty city street. "What do you have going on tonight? Another tattoo?"

"You aren't an ape, are you?" the crazy shirtless man said.

I had no idea how to reply.

"You aren't primitive. You have some instinct that the world that most people walk around in is merely a facade, that something different and darker is playing out just behind the curtain. You can feel that tingling all the way down in your cells, can't you?"

I remained silent. What was I supposed to say? The guy had clearly smoked up back at the motel.

"I mean, I don't really know what you mean," I finally said, speeding up a little more. Suddenly, I really needed the ride to end. "But, yeah, I've read some obscure stuff and seen some things around town that I wouldn't describe as normal."

My reply hung in the air, heavy, until I turned on to Holly and began to approach the tattoo parlor on the corner of Railroad.

"Pull into the red zone in front of the shop. I'm just picking something up," he said in that deep, muffled voice. "I'm going to tell you something before I go inside. If you don't think I'm crazy, I want you to wait for me. I won't be more than a few minutes, and I could use a ride to the Lighthouse Mission down the street."

I pulled into the red zone in front of a fire hydrant. My breath was growing strained with anxiety. Not about getting a ticket. But because I knew that my life was about to get a whole lot stranger and more complicated.

"Okay, what's up?" I asked, unable to turn to look at shirtless guy.

He studied me for a long time from behind the clunky metal bunny helmet. He could see my fear. He was probably having second thoughts about initiating me into his world.

"Have you ever heard of Azathoth?"

I glanced at the bunny helmet in the rearview mirror and reflexively pulled my mask aside to speak: "The H.P. Lovecraft elder god?"

The head inside the comically large helmet tried to nod.

"Yes. The eldest of the eldest. The slumbering chaos. The blind idiot god. He who weaves the worlds with his dreams. The gnawing shadow. The daemon sultan. Grandfather of the void and all things elder."

Shirtless guy was really pouring it on.

"Yeah, I've heard of him," I said, impatience tinging the tone of my voice as I snapped my mask back over my face.

"You know that if he wakes that reality will be destroyed? Even if he wakes for just a moment?"

I used to run a Call of Cthulhu group. I knew the deal and shirtless guy knew I knew.

"Yeah. Even if a 'shard' of him wakes. Whatever that means," I replied. "But doesn't he need cultists or something to awaken him?"

My stomach fell out my ass as realization set it.

"Wait," I said, snapping my agape jaw shut beneath my mask. "The homeless guys with the staves and clubs, the drummers…"

My voice trailed off just as the faint sound of primal drums began to grow from up the street, back the way we had just come.

Shirtless guy leapt into action at the sound. He was out of the minivan and racing into Old School just as an amorphous black mass up the street slowly transformed into a pack of bicycles in my side view mirror. The drumming was growing louder as the pack slowly rolled down the street. The streets were otherwise deserted.

Shirtless guy raced back out of the shop holding a wooden baseball bat. He pulled open the door and stuck his absurdly large bunny-helmet head into the van. I could see enough of the bat to tell it was covered in almost as many wards as shirtless guy. It stunk of soldering iron and burnt wood. It must have been getting modified while I was driving shirtless guy around town.

"Listen," he began in that deep, muffled voice. "Change of plans. I'll get to the mission on my own." His voice was urgent. He wasn't scared. He was taking command.

"You sure? I…"

He cut me off and tossed a one-hundred dollar bill at me. I stared dumbly at the money as the pack of cyclists began to whoosh by. I couldn't believe what I was seeing and hearing.

"Yes. I'm certain. Don't follow me. Things are going to get strange. And violent. You are not ready for it. I think I can handle this, but if I don't… If I fail…"

I was listening, but my eyes were on the cyclists. They weren't normal cyclists. They were grungy weirdos. Meth heads in cornrows and filthy homeless people with jail-house face tats. Many wore bandanas across their faces or masks with bizarre designs on them. Staves were strapped to their backs. Some held clubs. Several of them banged on drums mounted onto the steering wheels of their clearly stolen bicycles. But I knew they weren't merely transients. They were Doomsday Cultists, servitors of Azathoth the blind idiot god. They had come to Bellingham for only one reason: to awaken the slumbering chaos and destroy reality.

"Well, if I fail, it's just empty void anyway. But if things get too weird... If things get too dark and wonky, you understand, get your ass inside the Freemason Lodge on State Street."

The last of the pack was coming up on the minivan, banging out their drum beat.

"You understand?" shirtless guy demanded.

"Yeah, I know where that lodge is. I'll go there."

Shirtless guy's body was twitching. I know it doesn't make any sense, but it seemed like it was about to boil or something. Or like he was a rocket about to take off. Sounds nuts. I could describe it a half dozen different ways and it still wouldn't quite describe what I was seeing.

"I gotta go. Thank you for your kindness. Thank you for not being a blind ape."

With that, shirtless guy sprinted down the sidewalk. He was moving fast. Way too fast for a human, let alone a shoeless human. Blurry fast. He was easily catching up to the pack of cultists. On his bare feet. I could have sworn he lit up with a faint, emerald nimbus and grew a little bleary as he disappeared into the night. Totally nuts.

I turned off the engine and scooped up my earnings for the night. The cultists and shirtless guy were long gone down Holly Street, and I had no idea what to do besides try to process what I had just experienced over the previous hour. I could still hear the drum beat, but I wasn't sure if it was a mind worm or not.

I wasn't sure if I'd ever see shirtless guy again or if reality would even survive the night, so I slipped out of the minivan and into Old School. I slapped all my cash down on the counter as a squirrelly tattoo artist blinked at me.

"You with Doom Bunny?" the greasy-haired brunette asked.

"Who?" I asked back, genuinely confused.

"Guy you dropped off that just went running down the street. Doom Bunny," squirrely greasy guy stated.

"Yeah, kinda," I began. "Look, I need some tattoos. Do you do protection wards?"

Squirrely greasy guy shrugged: "I do all the wards, man. I created most of the ones Doom Bunny sports." He was snotty, and I wanted to punch him, but I needed to be okay with him. "I got a book in the back you can flip through."

"Cool," I said. "Let's start with a protection ward and see what else that stack of cash gets me afterwards."

I left Old School four hours later. The night was as still as I've ever known a night to be in Bellingham. Not a soul was to be found. No drums. The electricity in the air was gone. My car was unticketed. I winced at the rawness of the protection ward etched onto the inside of my wrist. It wasn't a proper ink tattoo. I don't know what that guy used, but it was raw, and it burned, and it was going to scar. I was able to afford a second ward. This second one was slightly larger, dead center on my chest. Squirrely greasy guy helped me select it and recommended I go a little bigger with it under the circumstances. He had one himself and shared it with me. It was intricate, not like any symbol I had ever come across. He said it helped maintain mental clarity and ward off insanity. Doom Bunny had mentioned a ward like that earlier. I figured if I was going to be any help to him keeping Bellingham safe from the minions of Azathoth, protection from going insane would be apropos.

I tossed the bottle of ointment squirrely greasy guy gave me next to a can of mace I kept in one of the many minivan compartments. The fresh tattoos stung so badly I was certain I'd use up the entire bottle in no time.

I turned on the engine and hung my mask over the rearview mirror. I considered turning on the Uber app and driving for a few more hours, but decided against it. I drove the silent street home, passing the red-brick Freemason Lodge along the way. It was only a block from my house. I could literally see it from my bedroom patio that overlooked a sizable chunk of downtown and Bellingham Bay. If I had to get to the lodge in a hurry, it wasn't going to be a problem. Judging by the lack of drum beats and a general sense of calm in the air, I assumed I wouldn't need to worry about that for the night.

Maybe I never would...but I was intent to find out why the lodges were safe from Azathoth and how Doom Bunny came to be a champion of Bellingham.

"And where Nyarlathotep went, rest vanished, for the small hours were rent with the screams of nightmare."

–H.P. Lovecraft

Lexi's Peril

Lexi's Peril *began as a kind of experiment in publishing for various serialized storytelling websites. The story was entered into and fortunate enough to place as a finalist in the TNT Top 100 Horror contest on Wattpad. It also led to a larger tale, one found on the Nightmare Alley channel as well as those aforementioned websites, called Legacy of the Wolf. Ultimately,* Lexi's Peril *is a story of courage. As for the father's voice... is it real or a child's subconscious helping to guide her through an impossible challenge? You be the judge.*

1. THE BULLET

Lexi Peterson found the bullet in a box of her dead father's things.

There had been a stack of magazines—Fish and Stream, Outdoor Life, Guns and Ammo, a canteen, some gun oil, papers, an old pair of binoculars—and that bullet. It was weird; shiny and smooth, same color as the heart pendant Dad had gotten her for her ninth birthday, just last year.

Outside, Chewy was barking his head off. From where she was sitting in the middle of the daylight basement floor, Lexi looked through the two windows set high in the east wall to the sky outside. It was almost full dark.

Just then Chewy's barking was overpowered by the sound of Tina yelling "shut up!" as loud as she could from the kitchen window.

Tina was Lexi's stepmom. Her real mom Felicia was in Poughkeepsie, half a world away. Her and Dad had gotten a divorce three years ago. There had been a lot of yelling and a ton of bad things were said by both mom and dad about each other. Mom did have some "challenges" that she was working through, like taking too many pills, even though they were prescribed by a doctor. And she drank. A lot. Either way, because of those things Dad ended up with full custody...

The farm they lived on belonged to her great uncle and aunt, Benji and Ruth. They were old, but a whole bunch of years ago they had a daughter of their own. She grew up and went to college so Lexi got to stay in her room. Dad got to stay in what used to be Ruth's craft room.

No matter what mom had said about him, Lexi thought her dad was... or, had been, the greatest: back when she was really little and couldn't stop crying because she lost her stuffed bunny, he told her it was okay... then he pretended to find it, even though she knew that he had gone out and bought a new one. He watched musicals on the kids' channel with her even though she was pretty sure he hated them. When she wanted to quit gymnastics because she totally sucked on the balance beam, he told her she could do it, that he believed in her, but he said the most important thing was for her to believe in herself. And when she still couldn't get the beam right he told her it was okay, that if she kept trying she would get it but no matter what he loved her. She was his little Bug-a-Lug.

He was a good dad. The best dad. The two of them were a team; he had always said so. And now he was gone. They were the Dynamic Duo, and he was gone. She would never see him again; never hear his voice unless it was from a recording; never wrap her arms around him...

Okay, no more crying. If she started, she wouldn't stop. Just like at the funeral. She wiped her nose on her sleeve and took a few deep, shaky breaths. Then she frowned, tilting her head to one side, listening.

Chewy had stopped barking.

Maybe Tina had gotten him in. Tina was okay. Lexi was actually starting to get used to her. But now that dad was... gone, she might end up going back to her real Mom. Benji and Ruth wanted Lexi to stay, along with Tina. That was why Benji and Ruth were gone- off to the city to talk to people in suits, and talk to mom, who had someone in a suit working for her (supposedly she had stopped drinking and taking pills), everybody deciding what would happen... and all Lexi could do was wait. Waiting was hard. But what was worse was not being in control of anything. Everything was happening *to* her. Her life had shattered like a glass house, coming down around her in pieces and there was nothing she could do but watch and wait. It wasn't fair! It wasn't fair...

It wasn't fair.

"Lexi!" a voice yelled. Lexi looked up to see Tina's shadow on the wall where the stairs turned. "Dinner in ten minutes! I'm gonna set the table and get Chewy in."

"Kay," she called back. The shadow disappeared. Time to put the box back where the others, the ones she had already gone through, were stacked, along the wall opposite the windows. But she didn't want to rush: closing this box felt a little bit like... closing out her dad.

Lexi looked back down at the bullet, held between her thumb and first finger. It was pretty, even though she knew how dangerous it was. Dad had taught her about guns. His job had been dangerous too. He was a marshal. He traveled all over the U.S. to catch bad guys. He didn't talk about his job much, except the month before he died. He had said that he was going after a whole family of bad people. Then he went away for a week, and when he came back he said he got 'em. The whole family, got 'em all. That night he snuggled with her extra tight while they watched TV. He had seemed sad. And the next night, when she was watching a scary movie on the cable channel, he came in and turned it off, right in the middle. When she asked why, dad had said "because the real world's scary enough."

A week after that they got the news. He had gone back out again and something terrible had happened. They wouldn't say how he died, only that it was "in the line of duty."

Don't cry, don't cry, don't cry...

She wiped her eyes, dropped the bullet back in the box and stood up. Her knees were sore from sitting cross-legged so long. As she stretched, Lexi looked out the windows. The moon was outside now, peeking up from the bottom of the window to her left. It was full, and it looked huge. She went and stood on the small wooden bench against the wall, staring out at that bright, big moon. It made her feel small. Lexi was wondering why the full moon always looked so ginormous just as it was coming up when she was startled by a long, loud scream.

2. GRAPE JUICE IN THE MOONLIGHT

That sound wasn't like anything she had ever heard, even in movies. It lasted for a long time before it was cut off, like someone hitting the stop button on a song right in the middle. Lexi's body stiffened; her hands flew over her mouth to hold in a cry of her own. Her wide eyes stared out the window at the giant moon.

If that yell came from Tina, she might be in trouble. And if she was in trouble, Lexi had to hurry...

She ran up the two flights of stairs and into the short hallway that led from the basement to the family room, past the tall window, through the living room to the entry where the front door was standing open.

The air was just starting to turn cold. Lexi stepped slowly out onto the front porch, her nose filled with the smell of alfalfa. Holding her hands tight together up in front of her chest, she took slow steps down the porch stairs.

To her right, she could see all the way to the main road. The long driveway ran from there past the front of the house and over to the carport on her left. Out beyond the driveway directly in front of her was nothing but empty, freshly-cut field, looking like a pale green ocean in the moonlight.

Stepping onto the driveway, Lexi peeked over at Tina's parked van. There was something on the ground on the other side; she could only see part of it, sticking out from the back wheel on the passenger side. She took a few more steps and saw that it was a person. A couple more short steps showed that it was Tina, on her back.

Lexi sucked in air. Tina's head was lying so that she faced Lexi. Her eyes were really, really wide. Her left arm was flopped out in Lexi's direction and her body from the chest down was hidden behind the van's tire and the shadowed ground. There were noises: crunching, ripping sounds. Tina's head moved up and down a little and her arm rolled back and forth.

"Tina?" Lexi said in a small, scared voice as she took another step. Something had spilled under Tina; the moonlight was shining on it; a black liquid like grape juice.

The noises stopped; Tina's body quit moving. A growl came from behind the van. Low and deep. Lexi felt it all the way through her chest like when you stood too close to a speaker, and she was scared that just the sound of it could make her heart stop. She looked closer at the liquid...

Not grape juice.

Blood.

Lexi screamed, turned and ran back up the steps. Something was coming out from behind the van, its feet sliding and then pounding on the gravel driveway. Lexi didn't want to look; couldn't look as she ran onto the porch and into the house, turned and shut the door and twisted the lock.

Something hit the front doors. Hard. Lexi fell back on her butt, screaming. She wanted dad— whenever she had been scared at night because of some noise or when she had a bad dream it was always dad who told her not to worry, that he wouldn't let anything *get* her.

The thing on the other side pounded against the door, scraping and pushing, trying to force its way in.

Dad was gone. Who would protect her now? She closed her eyes, rubbed the pendant around her neck and thought of his voice.

You're gonna be okay. You can get through this. I'm with you. You're a survivor.

That helped. Yes. The doors were thick. This thing, whatever it was, couldn't get in.

Even as she thought this the banging stopped. Lexi got up. She needed to get to the phone, call 911... she looked over as a shadow crossed the window in the living room. Whatever it was it was big— taller than the window. There and then gone. A phone...there was a phone in the family room, on one of the side tables by the couch.

Lexi walked through the living room toward the family room and stopped. The thing was standing at the tall window just across from her. Two glowing eyes. Yellow. Staring... and then its face moved closer. A nose, wet and black. Air came out of it and fogged the glass. When the fog cleared Lexi saw teeth. Long, white, pointed. And then it was gone. Moving on... to where? Around that side was just the wall, with the windows to the daylight basement, which were shut, past that the treehouse and the laundry room, and then the back of the house, the kitchen...

Lexi's chest clenched. The kitchen. During the summer both Ruth and Tina cooked with the kitchen window open.

She ran to close the window but only got as far as the short hall before stopping; there was a shredding sound coming through the hall as the monster tore at the kitchen screen.

It was getting in, and she couldn't stop it. If it got *into* the house... she would need to get *out*.

3. THE WOODSHED

The nearest neighbor was three miles away, and the workers wouldn't be back until morning. But... if she could get to the pole building out back, dad kept rifles there, in the gun safe—

Claws scraped against the sink. The thing in the kitchen hit the faucet handle. Water gushed.

The shortest way to the pole building was around the carport... which meant going near Tina...

You can do it. Run, sweetheart, run!

Lexi hurried back to the front doors, unlocked the right one and pushed, but neither door would move. They were all messed up from the monster hitting them. In the kitchen, feet or paws or whatever that thing had hit the tile floor. She took a step back and kicked. Once. Twice. Harder.

The right-side door finally broke open, just a few feet. She squeezed through and pushed the door shut as tight as she could but it wouldn't close all the way.

As she shuffled backward the thing inside the house hit the door and nearly broke through. Lexi screamed, turned and cleared the porch steps in one jump.

Behind her the doors cracked and splintered.

Go, baby girl, go!

The monster snarled; wood snapped as the doors gave way. Lexi ran as fast her feet would carry her, holding her left hand up to block her view as she sped past the van, past Tina, trying not to think of those eyes, staring but seeing nothing; nothing anymore forever.

She could hear the monster running fast on the gravel— too fast. There was no way she could make the pole building in time. Far to her right was the hay barn—too far away—but directly in front of her was the wood shed.

Lexi ran up the little ramp, flung open the door, stepped on the first small piles and then climbed onto the higher ones. There was just enough space between these and the roof for her to crawl over.

The little shed was dusty and old, really old; long and made of planks and shaped like a strange, tiny house with sides that went up and out toward the top; like something out of a cartoon. She had snuck into it once when her and dad had played hide and seek and gotten into trouble—Dad said she could hurt herself because the wood could collapse or she would get splinters.

Suddenly the whole place shook. Lexi pulled wood from either side and dropped it behind her feet. The air felt thick and it was getting hard to breathe but she forced herself further in.

There was a low growl in the dark; that same sound that vibrated her chest. In between the monster sounds were the loud, desperate gasps of her own breathing. Her plan—as silly a plan as it was—was to hope that the monster would try to crawl in after her and get stuck.

She continued on, squeezing as tight as she could, going further, deeper. The thing in the dark clawed at the logs. The pile beneath her shifted; Lexi scrambled and felt a long sliver of wood jab through her jeans into her left thigh and then snap off as she kept pushing forward. Suddenly it felt as though everything was closing in on her.

The woodpile moved again; glancing over her shoulder Lexi spotted glowing eyes before a claw snagged the back of her right shoe.

Lexi yanked her foot upward. The shoe came off, and she squirmed as fast as she could all the way to the back of the shed. Now she would find out if she was right about something: the boards the shed was made of; about how old and rotted they were... mustering every bit of strength she had, Lexi punched the back wall and heard wood creak.

Harder! Give it all you got!

Beneath her, the pile moved again, along with the sounds of logs further back rolling, knocking together as the thing cleared a path.

With grunts of effort Lexi hit the wall board again and again, as hard as she possibly could. It gave a little bit each time until finally it broke and a piece fell away. The space she had made was barely enough for her to get through but she held her breath, stuck her head out first and then kicked and struggled (expecting any second for a clawed hand to latch onto her ankle and pull her back into the darkness) until her chest and finally the rest of her was out and she fell onto the grass, air rushing from her lungs with the impact.

She sucked in breath and scrambled back as a clawed, fur-covered hand lunged out from the space in the upper back wall of the shed. It swiped at the air. Lexi got up, trying her best to ignore the burning pain in her left thigh and the awkwardness of having one shoe, she ran, looking back—

Then tripped, landing hard on the grass, numbing her left shoulder. She rolled and looked down to see what it was she tripped over... and screamed at the sight of a torn-up mound of meat and fur and insides. She knew, even though she couldn't recognize him, that this was all that was left of Chewy.

Not fair. Like so many other things, it just wasn't fair. Benji and Ruth's beloved family dog... gone forever. Just like dad. Just like Tina.

Boards flew from the shed's back wall into the grass. Slowly, the monster began pulling itself out.

Lexi rubbed at her pendant.

I'm here, sweetheart, I'm with you. I know you're tired but you have to keep running.

She wiped her eyes, got up and did exactly that.

4. HUNTER AND HUNTED

Like everything else on the farm, the pole building was old. As she ran in, flipped on the light and closed the side door behind her, she knew that the thin wood wouldn't keep the monster out.

But all she needed was enough time to open the gun safe and load the rifle. The safe was at the back of the big garage-like structure. She hurried around Benji's boat—his pride and joy, a Bayliner, sitting on top of a trailer with its nose pointed toward the rollup door-across the floor to the safe and began working the combination. On her first try she failed because her hands were shaking so bad.

Slow down, Bug-a-Lug. Breathe.

Dad had hated locking up his rifles but Benji and Ruth had insisted. And they wouldn't let him keep them in the house. Maybe that would end up being a good thing. If she could just get to them...

A cracking, splintering sound came from the other end of the building. The monster was smashing its way through.

You can do this.

She tried the combination again, slower this time, and got it.

Just as she heard the wooden door give way, Lexi grabbed the closest rifle, what dad had called a "bolt action." A low growl came from inside the open space, bouncing off the metal walls. Lexi's heart beat fast and hard and her throat nearly closed up.

She snatched up a loaded magazine from a small shelf in the safe.

On the other side of the boat, Lexi could hear the thing's feet on the gravel, one step at a time. It was a crunkly sound, like someone stepping on corn flakes.

Crnk, crnk, crnk-

The rifle wasn't loaded yet. Lexi slammed the magazine into the stock, pulled the bolt back and then shoved it forward again to load the first bullet.

Crnk, crnk-

Safety. She had to check the safety! She looked and flipped it down to the "fire" position. Swinging the rifle butt to her shoulder Lexi aimed at the back of the boat where the thing would appear any second...

Crnk.

Silence. Lexi waited, her breaths coming loud and fast as she held the heavy rifle in place. Where was it? The cabin on the back of the boat was tall enough that she couldn't see. The boat *was* on a trailer, so if she got down really low she'd be able to peek under but if that thing came running she wouldn't get the weapon raised in time...

Lexi took a step forward. The rifle was shaking now. Her shoulders were sore, burning. But she knew she couldn't lower that weapon. Lowering it could mean death.

Another step. She tried to quiet her own breathing so she might here the monster, but there was only the eerie quiet. One more step and she'd be able to see most of the open space on the other side of the Bayliner. But the rifle was getting so heavy. She was gritting her teeth and even in the cool air she had started to sweat. One more step...

There was a thud! Next to her, the back of the boat *dropped* by an inch.

On the boat oh God it's on the boat it's-

Lexi skittered backward on her heels, into the building's back wall, looking up. The thing was on top of the cabin, holding onto a piece that went up at an angle like the metal parts next to the windshield of a car. It was dark against the hanging fluorescent light, eyes like yellow stars, hunched over, patches of thick black fur poking from its shoulders. The claws on its hand were long, dark and sharp, scraping paint from the metal as the hand tightened. That low rumbling came from its throat, the lips pulled from its teeth as its head lowered. The body became tense, the way a cat's would just before it leaped.

Shoot! Shoot!

Lexi fired.

The sound of the rifle was deafening. It kicked against her shoulder and gun smoke filled her nostrils. The bullet hit the thing in the chest, blasting it off of the boat. Its dark form disappeared and landed on the other side with a heavy thump.

Lexi's ears were ringing. But... she did it! She hit it. It was dead, it had to be.

But what if it wasn't?

Lexi yanked the bolt back, ejecting the shell from the last round, then slammed it forward, loading the next. Taking quick steps she came around to where she could see the other side...

The monster was there, lying in a heap. Unmoving.

Letting out a huge breath, Lexi lowered the rifle and rubbed at her right shoulder. Tears streamed down her cheeks.

It was over. Now she just needed to go call 911. She didn't want to walk right past it, not that close, and the only ways in and out of the building were the side door and rolling door.

Slinging the rifle onto her shoulder, Lexi walked around the back of the boat to the other side and then around the front. She took one last look at the thing, the thing that shouldn't exist (*the world's scary enough already*) before hurrying through the doorway, trying not to step on the ruined door's jagged splinters with the foot that was missing a shoe.

The air had grown colder outside, cooling the sweat on Lexi's skin. She felt awkward walking, with the one shoe missing and her thigh killing her where the splinter from the woodshed had gone in. Straight ahead of her was the back door that led into the laundry room. She hurried toward it, heading up the steps, although she was pretty sure it was—

Locked. Although Benji and Ruth never locked their doors, Tina and Dad always did. Lexi turned, winced from the pain in her thigh as she went back down the steps and-

Froze.

That growl. That low sound like an old car engine.

It was back.

There was a rectangle of light from shining out the side of the pole building, from the doorway onto the ground. A shadow stepped into that square of light, a shadow that was part animal, part man. Its feet crunched on the busted wood. The shadow moved...

And the thing's hand appeared around the corner of the building, those dark claws grasping. The head came around next, eyes glowing like the headlights of an oncoming truck.

5. THE SAFE PLACE

This isn't over yet sweetheart. Dig deep. Think.

Just around the corner to her left was the treehouse.

Lexi ran. The monster let out a sound somewhere between a bark and shout, and charged.

Benji had built the treehouse for his daughter many, many years ago. Dad had double checked it for safety and once it had checked out Lexi played in it and loved it; it was her safe place.

Within just a few steps she was there at the base of the tree. The structure wasn't fancy. It was pretty small, built high in the branches of an old hickory. There were spaced-apart wood planks nailed to the trunk that made a ladder. Lexi climbed as fast as she could, hearing thudding footfalls getting louder. And closer... Lexi tossed open the trapdoor in the bottom of the treehouse and pulled herself in. When she looked back down, the monster was there; its eyes and teeth bright in the moonlight as she scooted over, dragging the rifle, and slammed the trapdoor closed.

Over the past few years, when her cousins spent weekends on the farm, Lexi and the girls would play in the treehouse and make the boys stay out unless they knew the secret password, which changed depending on whether or not the girls wanted the boys around. If the girls wanted the boys locked out, they took a thick piece of wood and slid it through two big staples, one on the trapdoor and one set into the floor. Lexi slid this piece of wood through the staples now and backed into the corner of the tiny shack.

A little voice in the back of her mind, that same voice in gymnastics that told her she would fall when she was walking the balance beam, told her now that it was hopeless; that she should just give up. There was no way to kill this thing. Instead, it was going to kill her...

But then she remembered the movie she had been watching— the scary movie, when Dad had come in and turned it off. It was about a wolf-man, and in that movie the wolf-man could only be killed with silver bullets.

Lexi thought of the box with her dad's things in it, and she thought of the shiny bullet she had found there.

Suddenly the entire structure rocked as the thing slammed into the trap door, kicking up dust and splitting boards amid sharp cracking sounds.

It wouldn't take long for the monster to get in... to destroy her safe place.

To *get* her.

Lexi thought hard. Since she had moved in to the upstairs room there were times when she had leaned on the sill and looked out her window at the treehouse, imagining what it might be like to walk the large branch that stuck out from the hickory's side and pointed toward her room, thinning just before angling up above her window to lay a few inches over the eaves. Sometimes, when it stormed really bad, she could hear that branch scraping the roof.

What if she could get onto that branch, and use it to get to her window? The window was big, the kind that slid sideways...

The thing hit the floor again, making her yelp. The wood snapped and splintered. One more good hit and the monster would be through.

Even if she could get to her window, it was closed, how could she-

And then she remembered the rifle. Of course...

There was a small window in the treehouse which looked out onto that branch. Lexi positioned herself on her knees, stuck the barrel out the treehouse window and tucked the rifle butt to her shoulder. She aimed... down where the light from the hallway shown into her room. Forcing herself to control her breath, she fired.

Her already-sore shoulder hurt even more from the rifle's kick and her ears rang, but she heard glass shatter... just as the floor behind her came apart.

Working the bolt again, Lexi pulled the rifle barrel out from the window and swung it over. She put her back against the wall. The last time she had shot this monster, at least it had been stunned for a minute. The beast was halfway through the ruined trap door, reaching for her. She aimed right at that face, right between those glowing animal eyes and she pulled the trigger.

The thing's head jerked backward. The body went limp and the head came forward again, dropping down onto the floor.

Lexi pushed the rifle out the small window, butt first, getting ready to climb out, and then stopped. When she had thought about using the branch before, she always imagined having to walk it where it got thick near the treehouse... just like the balance beam.

And in her mind she had always fallen. The branch was big, but not big enough to crawl on. She would have to stand until it started to thin, and then she would have to hang from it and swing...

You can do this, baby girl. You just have to believe in yourself.

The thing behind her took in a deep breath. Live, or die, this was it. Time to "put up or shut up," as dad would say. But as silly as it sounded, in some ways, Lexi was more scared of walking that branch than she was of the wolf-man.

She heard its arm drag across the wood. If she was going to go for it, it had to be now.

Only having one shoe would throw her off, so she took off the other one. Socks too— she could get better grip with her bare feet. Then, through the opening she climbed, one hand holding onto the thin window ledge as she put the rifle strap back on her shoulder and stood shakily on the branch.

6. THE WINDOW

You have to hurry.

But she couldn't... because she would fall. And it was so far down. She would fall and break her legs or her back and then she wouldn't be able to move and that thing would come for her and the last thing she would see would be its teeth...

Cracking noises sounded from the structure, along with that low growl. It was coming, and she had to move.

Lexi took one step, teetered and then took another, arms spread out at her sides.

Don't stop, keep going!

Another step, but too fast. It threw her off and she bent sideways at the waist, one arm down, the other arm, the one with the rifle strapped to it, flung up, tilting, too far, too far...

That hand caught a tiny, hanging limb above, no bigger around than her pinkie, but enough to pinch and stop her lean. Her upper body straightened back up. She couldn't keep hold of that limb and keep moving, so she let it go, took another step...

You're doing it! You're doing great, Baby Girl, just—

A deafening series of barks and snarls erupted behind her, making her jump, and suddenly she was balancing on one foot, her upper body swaying first one direction, then the other. She could hear those teeth snapping as the monster jammed its head through the small opening. Lexi's heart felt like it would jump right out of her chest. Forcing her body weight forward enough to bring her other foot back down on the branch, she was able to get her balance back. She took one more step; the branch, which had begun to thin, lowered a few inches as its other end made a scratching sound on the roof.

The beast thrashed against the treehouse wall around the window; smashing, breaking, shaking the branch. Lexi was going to fall...

Bending her knees she dropped down and back onto her butt, then sat forward with one leg to either side, her hands grasping the wood that was about as big around as the end of a baseball bat. The rifle strap had fallen to her wrist, cutting into her skin.

The wall behind her was cracking, snapping. The wolf-man was breaking through. Lexi leaned fully forward; her window was just a few feet away and not too far down...

Maneuvering sideways, Lexi leaned on the branch with straight arms, swung her left leg over and was balancing now on her stomach. Looping her hand under the branch she slipped down, the rough bark lifting her shirt and scraping her tummy...

Until at last she was suspended, hanging with one hand holding the branch on either side, legs kicking at empty air, the rifle strap back now at her shoulder. Grunts of exertion escaped her; sweat dripped into her eyes as she walked one hand over the other, as fast as she could, knowing that if she stopped for too long her grip would give. Taking one desperate look up and behind, Lexi saw those bright eyes, moving through what remained of the treehouse wall, lowering its head as its claws wrapped around the thickest part of the branch.

The other end of the branch, the part that angled up, had lowered to where the straight part of it stopped just under the eaves of her window. Lexi walked her hands a few more inches, her fingers ready to give out any second. The good news was she was close enough to swing...

But there was a problem. One big problem. When she had shot the glass, the bullet had left a hole, with spider web cracks that went out in all directions, but the window was still in one piece. She would have to swing, kick it with her feet...

She took one swing, kicked, and felt her fingers slip the tiniest bit as her feet bounced off the glass. It had cracked in more places but didn't come apart.

Harder! You have to kick harder! Give it all you got.

Lexi swung and kicked as hard as she could. Huge pieces of glass fell away onto the carpet of her bedroom. But one jagged point of it, six inches long, had stayed. It jutted up from the bottom like a knife blade, waiting to slice right through her if she didn't get the timing or the angle of her drop right.

The branch moved. That thing was crawling and the growl was so close it vibrated the insides of her ears. She was on the backswing and her fingers had all but given out. She wouldn't get another chance at this.

Your mind will tell you can't do it, but you can, sweetheart. You have to: and you have to do it now.

Lexi swung forward and as her feet passed through the window's open space her grip finally gave out; her body flew out and down, and the tip of that jagged shard of glass ran up and through her waving hair, less than an inch from the back of her skull.

She landed hard on the carpet and some of the bigger pieces of glass. They cracked but didn't break as far as she could tell. The barrel of the rifle had smacked into the side of her head and it hurt like hell.

But she was alive.

I knew you could do it, baby girl. And I know you're in pain and I know you're tired but you're almost out of this. Just hang tough for a little bit longer...

She had to keep moving. Smaller pieces of glass jabbed into her left palm as she used it get to her knees, reaching to the corner of her bed, pulling herself to her feet... her bare feet which were also now getting cut by pieces of glass that felt like hundreds of little insect bites. Lexi gritted her teeth and tried to step where it looked like there was no glass on the floor.

After three painful steps toward the light of the hallway she heard a loud crack followed by a thundering crash.

The branch had broken and hopefully both it and the monster had fallen to the ground.

Lexi smiled a little, hoping the fall hurt.

Then she remembered the front door, the door that the wolf-man had smashed through and her blood turned cold. If the beast was on the ground outside, it would come around to the front door, and if it came into the house before she could get to the bullet...

Run Lexi, run!

7. ONE SHOT

The first few steps were so painful Lexi thought she would just pass out, that everything would go black and then the monster would come in and do to her what it had done to Tina, to Chewy...

But after those first steps, her mind found a way to block out the pain. Or maybe her body just became numb to it. Either way, she was on the move—through the second floor hall to the staircase, then down one turn of stairs, then down the last turn, which opened onto the family room. She was rushing from the bottom of the staircase toward the short hall to the basement when the beast crashed through what remained of the front doors.

She didn't dare look behind her; could only imagine the wolf-man speeding closer and closer, claws reaching out to grab and pull her back, where those teeth would be waiting...

Lexi raced through the short hall to the basement door, still open from when she had left. She darted into the doorway and she could actually *smell* the monster-a smell like hickory and alfalfa and kind of like Chewy— as it passed within inches of her, moving too fast to stop and change direction.

It was only a split second, but it was long enough for Lexi to shut the door. While the door rocked in its frame she sped down the two sets of stairs to the daylight basement, back to where she had been when she first heard Tina scream, when this whole crazy nightmare began. The gnawing sensation in her feet had come back even worse than before as the glass pieces worked their way further into the bottoms of her feet, but she was so close. So close.

The box was there in the middle of the floor where she had left it. She positioned herself on the box's other side so she could see the stairs, dropped to her knees, slid the rifle off her right arm and began rummaging.

Upstairs, wood cracked and split. Not seeing the bullet immediately, Lexi turned the box over, tossing the magazines and the papers and the canteen aside...

And there it was, shining in the overhead light.

The door burst to pieces.

Lexi snatched up the rifle, hit the button to eject the magazine, pulled the bolt back. The old casing flew out.

The beast took the first set of stairs in one big jump, so big that it smashed into the wall at the turn, ending up stuck, half inside the wall and half outside...

Lexi looked at the bullet— the size of it. She hadn't thought about it before but she had to hope now that it was the right size. The right... what was it dad called it? Caliber? It would work. It had to work. She dropped the silver bullet into the chamber, shoved the bolt forward and down...

You can do this. I love you.

The wolf-man pulled itself out of the wall and crouched on the landing, staring with its yellow eyes, eyes that seemed to say this was it; her time was up; that she was nothing more than meat to warm its belly.

"No I'm not," Lexi said out loud in a strong, steady voice.

She thought of all the things in her life that she couldn't control; all the things that weren't fair, all the things that were happening around her and *to* her... enough was enough. This was it: one bullet, one shot, one chance to take *back* control of her life.

She lifted the rifle.

The beast leapt.

Lexi pulled the trigger.

The weight of the monster crashed down on her, driving the breath from her lungs. She waited for biting and the clawing, waited for the end... but nothing came. A rattle escaped the thing's throat but other than that it didn't move or make a sound.

Enough of her left leg and arm were out from underneath the wolf-man that she could use them to push the rest of her out, leaving the rifle behind. She scooted away, staring at the quarter-size hole in the thing's back. The center of its back; on the other side of where its heart would be.

Scooting further, to the base of the stairs, she kept an eye on the monster. It still didn't move. Slowly, she forced herself to stand.

And then, something strange happened. The skin of the thing began to... ripple. Like waves. Like there were bugs underneath trying to get out. The thing shifted and jerked and Lexi's heart caught, as she thought at first that it was coming back again, but this was different. There were snapping sounds. The legs with the knees that went backwards cracked, popped and repositioned. The fur covering the wolf-man went the other way, like it was growing in reverse, going back into the skin. Soon, what was there was a man, lying on his belly with his head sideways.

He was naked, which was gross, but she took two painful steps to the side, toward the boxes against the wall. She had to see its face. She had to know what this man looked like, this man who killed Tina and Chewy and almost killed her.

Two more steps and she could see that face. The eyes were open. They were the eyes of a stranger. The face was not a face she knew. Dark eyes, black hair.

Lexi thought back to when dad had started acting strange, talking about how scary the world was... that happened not long after he had talked about the bad people, and how he had gotten them all; the whole family...

But what if he had been wrong? What if he hadn't gotten all of them, and this thing, this stranger, was the one who killed her dad... and then he came after *his* family, to get back at him?

Maybe. Maybe that was what happened, maybe not. Maybe Lexi would never know.

What she did know was that she was alive. Tired, and hurting, but alive. She reached into her shirt and pulled out the silver pendant dad bought her for her birthday and she held it tight.

I couldn't be more proud of you, Bug-a-Lug. I love you, more than anything in the world. I always did, and I always will. My heart and my soul live on inside of you, my beautiful Baby Girl.

And then the voice was gone. But Lexi knew that she hadn't heard it for the last time. It would be there, when she needed it most.

No matter what, after tonight, Lexi knew that no matter how bad things got...

She could survive anything.

Porkus

Porkus, *along with* Room C6, *was the premiere episode on the Nightmare Alley channel. It is Creepypasta at its finest and written in a voice specific to that internet genre. Half-man, half-pig, 100% homicidal intention. If Porkus comes knocking, you better get your affairs in order.*

I'm not much of a writer. I'm terrified for my life—and I don't even know who I'm writing this for—but I have to put these words down.

Let me start over. Let me start at the beginning...

My younger years were not exactly happy ones. My mom had problems. Drugs. I often found myself alone in whatever we were calling a home at the time or in a car in a strange parking lot. One night when I was about 5, I'm guessing, she left me alone in her crap green station wagon. The kind with the fake wood paneling. I was tiny and it was huge. Even if it wasn't for the events that began that night, my little brain would have remembered it vividly. I was barely more than a baby, but I have memories dating back further. It's a little unusual, but not unheard of. Especially for kids that suffered early childhood trauma and neglect.

It was cold and foggy. I think we were living in Port Angeles at the time. It's right on the ocean in the Pacific Northwest, so cold, wet, and foggy were pretty common. I don't remember what my mom told me she was doing. I just remember that she told me to wait in the car, don't open the door for anyone, and that she'd be right back. She had parked under a street light. I only remember that because the light was on the fritz and periodically flicked on and off. I also remember that she was gone for a long time, long enough for me to have been worrying for a while.

My little breath was starting to steam up the windows as time went on. I occupied my time flipping through my tiny collection of battered baseball cards, but it was dark and the flickering light wasn't much help. It was then that something large walked past the car. Really close. At first I thought it was just the flickering street lamp, but I had felt something brush up against the puke green car paneling. The windows were steamed up and beading with moisture. It was impossible to see anything outside the car except large, vague shapes.

I was about to use the sleeve of my tattered sweatshirt to wipe at the window when I felt something bump the car. No, more like shake it. With purpose. Someone was outside—and it knew someone was inside.

My heart beat painfully in my chest. I was just a little boy. It was all I could do to not pee myself. All my instincts screamed at me to stay as still and silent as possible. Eventually it would go away. That's when I heard something scratching the surface of the car. A knife or something metallic was sliding along the car paneling. Something really sharp. It was growing louder as it neared the passenger-side door where I sat. I was so scared that I was certain whoever it was outside could hear my heart pounding and my short sips of panicked breath. I know now that I was on the verge of hyperventilating. I had no idea what I was experiencing.

I risked a look out the side window. Whatever it was outside the car was standing at the passenger door. Just...standing. Every time the street light flickered, its hulking silhouette was illuminated through the steamed-up window.

Just then a rap came at the window and I let out a little scream. I'd realize later that I had pissed myself. I shouldn't be embarrassed by this; I was just a little boy. But it's not a memory I like to dwell on.

The rap at the window came again.

I don't know why, but I reached out and wiped at the steamed window with the sleeve of my sweater so I could see who the person was. I'll never forget what I saw.

Standing a few paces back from the door was something that was humanoid but not quite human: a bipedal creature that was more wild boar than man. Its arms and legs were human. It stood erect like a man. The torso? The head? Fully wild boar. Its feet where huge, shoeless, hairy, and gnarly. The nails were more claws than what you and I would expect on a humanoid hand.

I was paralyzed with terror. What was this thing? What did it want? Why was it just staring at me with its beady pig eyes? I'll never forget those eyes. They stared at and through me, completely alien and unreadable.

I have no idea how much time passed, me staring at the pig man in the flickering streetlight and it staring back at me. But every detail of its body has been seared into my memory: Its umber, leathery skin; the massively muscled arms; its big pig-like belly; the oily leather pants; the constant sniffing of its snout; the clawed hands and feet; and the long, well-worn tusks that grew out from the side of its face. Who could ever forget something like that, even if it was glimpsed for only an instant?

It was then that another car entered the parking lot on the far side from where I was trapped by the pig man. I looked hopefully in the car's direction as its headlights slid over the exterior of the station wagon and briefly illuminated the interior. Maybe mom was inside. It was then that I turning back to the passenger window. I let out a little screech. The pig man was staring in at me, bent over. Snout nearly touching the glass. The pig man's beady eyes stared directly at me. There was no mistaking the homicidal menace in those eyes. I watched as it held up its clawed hand and it ticked off a count of three with its fingers. With the other hand, it made a slicing motion across its bloated, leathery throat.

The other car was inching closer. I dared a look out of a half moon of clear glass out the front window of the car, down where the window met the dashboard. Suddenly, the pig man banged at the passenger window to get my attention back. Its snout let out a blast of air. It was loud and primal and immediately steamed up the window from the outside.

I could no longer see the pig man. Was the nightmare over? Was he just going to go away? Fade away in the mist and flickering darkness of the night? I was panting and could see the little puffs of breath I was making but I couldn't take my eye off the steamed-up window. Just then, one of its huge fingers dragged down the window, screeching as it wrote the number "1."

And then it was over. My mom showed up not long after that and scolded me for peeing myself. I was too scared to talk to her about what I saw. I never told her about it, but I never looked at those baseball cards again and I never let her leave me alone in a parking lot ever again. I would occasionally doodle the pig man on my school work until my first grade teacher, Ms. Green, got concerned and had me talk to a counselor. The counselor asked me what the pig man was and why I needed to draw it so often. I was a tight lipped little shit. I just shrugged and said, "I don't know. It's just Porkus."

I repressed the memory for years. It wasn't too long after that that my grandparents got custody of me and not too much longer after that that I lost my mom to whatever drugs she spent all her time and money on. Doodling Porkus abruptly halted. Years passed and I grew into what I thought was a relatively normal adult with a family. I had a good job and we owned our home.

When I was 28, my now ex-wife and I lived in a split level home just off the suburban beaten path in Redmond. We had a short driveway and the house was surrounded by lots of trees. It was another wet, cold Pacific Northwest night. I had just taken the garbage cans out to the curb and was going about my normal evening routine of securing the house before heading to bed. My wife and little boy where already asleep. I was walking through the living room when I heard one of the cans—they were still made of galvanized metal back then—crash to the ground and the lid being banged about. It didn't sound like raccoons to me, so my thoughts went immediately to neighbor boys.

I went to the darkened bay window of the living room that overlooked the driveway. I was more annoyed than anything—until I saw what I thought I would never see again. Porkus. The pig man from my childhood. It shouldn't have been able to see me in the darkened window, but it was clearly staring directly up at me, holding a garbage can lid in one hand. More than 20 years had passed, but it looked exactly the same as it did that night in the parking lot. Surely it couldn't see me, I thought to myself. As if to answer my question, the creature kicked at the garbage strewn at its feet and beat the galvanized lid against the garbage can it had not knocked over.

To make it perfectly clear that it could see me, it pointed at me with one clawed finger.

Suddenly, I was filled with the same paralyzing terror that had gripped me all those years ago when I was just a 5 year-old boy. What did this thing want? How did it find me? How was I going to protect my family from it? Fortunately, I was no longer a little boy. I stepped away from the bay window and returned to the front door. I turned on the floodlights that illuminated much of my yard.

My wife and the handy man I had hired to do the install thought the lights were excessive. I knew they weren't. I double checked to ensure the alarm system was activated. I had just walked the interior perimeter of my home to ensure we were properly locked in for the evening, but I retraced my steps regardless. Finally, I found myself in the kitchen dialing 911.

As I dialed, I heard an all-to-familiar rap on nearby glass. I frantically searched the kitchen and adjoining dining-room windows. A strange shape filled the corner of my eye and my heart leapt into my chest. I turned in the direction of the shape towards the sliding glass door. Standing just outside the door was Porkus. I nearly dropped the phone, and may have done just that had an operator not picked up at that moment.

"Please state the nature of your emergency," came the female voice.

I remember speaking, rushed and nervous and telling the operator that there was a trespasser on my property. I told her I had reason to believe that he meant us harm. But I don't remember saying the words precisely. I was too transfixed on Porkus. He was no more than 5 feet in front of me. The only thing standing between him and me—and ultimately my family—was a thin pane of glass. The pig man was powerfully built. I had no doubt it could easily break into my flimsy little fortress and tear me to shreds with those claws and tusks.

It just stood there staring at me with its beady eyes, radiating homicidal intent, then it lifted a hand and ticked off a count of three. Those fingers were every bit as big and clawed as I remembered from my childhood. Then it made a slashing motion with its other hand across its throat. Exactly in the same manner as I remembered.

Just as it did when I was a boy, it brought its snout to the glass and exhaled a loud, primal blast of air. A patch of glass steamed up. I stood there staring at it. I was stammering, trying to answer the 911 operator's questions as the pig man drew two fingers down the fogged-up glass. I had no idea what it was trying to communicate. I fumbled through the conversation with the operator a few seconds longer and was assured an officer was on the way. But of course by the time the officer arrived and my wife had been woken, the pig man had disappeared. I had no idea how to explain to them what had actually occurred, that Porkus had returned. The truth was not an option.

My need for security and over-protectiveness of my family blossomed into a full-blown disorder from that moment on. My wife forced me into therapy, but I could never really talk about what was happening. I knew that Porkus wanted to kill me, but why? What had it been doing in the intervening years? Why the fixation with the number "3"? Would it harm my family when it finally did come for me? I never found out. My wife left me after a few years of unsuccessful counseling. I've grown apart from my only child over the last few decades.

I'm 54 now. I'm writing this from my cabin on Lopez Island. I've been holed up here with my bug out bag and a shotgun I don't really know how to use. I saw Porkus again at my condo in Westlake. I watched him through the security camera. He stared right into the camera. How he knew it was mine or that I'd watch the video is beyond me. But he did. He held up three clawed fingers and made the throat slashing gesture.

I had plenty of time over the decades to come to understand what he was telling me. He would visit me three times. On the third visit, he would kill me. The visit at Westlake was the last time he would come to me and let me live. It took next to no time after watching that video for me to grab my bug out bag and hop from Seattle to Lopez on a charter plane.

I have no idea why the pig man has haunted me all these years. Or if it does the same to others. Its motivations are its own. I just know that typing these words may be my last act before he comes for me. Maybe this laptop will survive Porkus's attack on me and someone will find this document. Maybe it could help someone else who may be tormented by this monster. Regardless, it's written and I doubt I'll ever write anything ever again. Wait. What was that sound? Is something rapping on the window of the front door?

Room C6

Room C6 was born of frustration with ignorance, intolerance and hypocrisy. The fictional church of Dartmoor in the story is based on a despicable organization that is, unfortunately, all too real, though they receive less publicity nowadays than they did years ago. Nevertheless, recent events have shown that ignorance, intolerance and hypocrisy all continue to flourish. The story's champion, the answer to these ancient evils, is Vindicator. This begs the question: If you could command your own Vindicator, would you? If so, what would you have it do? Also worth thinking about: If others could direct their own Vindicator, would they use it against you?

J ust past midnight, Tommy heard chains dragging on the tile floor.

The noise came from outside the room and down the hall: clinking, dragging, getting closer. Three rooms down. Then two. Then one...

Something waited at the door. He hid against the opposite wall, knees to his chest. A shadow appeared under the door but it was quickly obscured by... mist. No, smoke. Drifting in through the narrow space. It billowed and rolled toward him as if driven by an unseen intelligence, carrying with it a scent that he recognized, vaguely; frankincense? Myrrh? He couldn't remember. He couldn't remember much of anything.

A piercing sound: metal on metal. The thing outside wanted in but the door was locked.

That was, after all, what you did with crazy people. Lock them up and throw away the key. And Tommy was most definitely crazy.

Wasn't he?

He closed his eyes and tried to remember...

The troubles had started years ago when Tommy's older brother Kent was still in high school.

It was an awkward time for Kent. In many ways he was still trying to figure out who he was; what his preferences were. He had kissed a boy after the football game and the news had spread. The local church, Dartmoor, had gotten word of it and they initiated a campaign on social media, warning that God would punish him. They said the earth would be cleansed of sodomites. They said Kent would incur God's wrath.

Dartmoor was a Baptist church, but the Baptists had denounced them. They were known to be a hate group. Most of their so-called congregation were members of the same inbred family. They were a black mark on the community, and most everyone in the small town knew that and kept them at arm's length.

Eventually the media assault subsided. Kent went on with his life. He joined the Army... and less than a year later he died, in Afghanistan. Tommy and the rest of the family had nearly forgotten about Dartmoor until the day of the funeral.

They protested Kent's funeral. Standing on the road outside the cemetery with signs that announced "God hates America" and "God hates homos." Tommy's dad Lance punched one of them. The police intervened but said the church was within its rights. "What about Kent's rights?" dad had screamed...

Tommy opened his eyes. Back in the room, back in the here and now. There was no smoke. No sound of sliding chains. Had he imagined it? Dreamed it? He didn't always know what was real anymore.

He forgot what he had been thinking about. The funeral... and... after. What had happened after? His memory clouded once again. He tried to think, but it was hard. He sat on his bed, back against the wall.

There were no windows here; no handle on the inside of the door. There was only the bed and the toilet. The walls were cushioned. It was a punishment, because Tommy had "acted out." The next step, they said, would be a straightjacket.

He tried to remember the incident. Was it yesterday? The day before? He had attacked another patient. The skinny man with wild eyes and rotten teeth. He had come so close that Tommy could smell his rancid breath and he said "Lack o' parental supervision, that's the trouble, see? Boy needs his daddy! Daddy keep you in line, son! Bend you over his knee and—" and that was when Tommy had attacked him, pushed him to the ground, pounded his chest and face. The men in white had stopped him before any real damage had been done, but it was enough. Enough to get him sent to the "personal safety room."

Had he slept? He thought so but he couldn't be sure. Maybe sleep would help.

He laid down and soon felt a soft rumbling through the metal bed frame. If he listened closely he could hear the sleeper train blowing its whistle, like it did every night. Before the chains and the smoke.

Midnight. Always at midnight.

Sleep. Get some sleep, he thought. But then it happened again. The sound of the chains, getting louder. Tommy sat up, got to his knees and watched; waited. A shadow again, under the door. Smoke coming through, carpeting the floor, and beneath it… movement. The floor came alive. And then he saw them, scurrying up the walls: bugs. Beetles and cockroaches, spiders, centipedes, millipedes, and freakish insects he couldn't even put a name to. Tommy was terrified of bugs, always had been. He scooted back on the bed as they closed in on him from every direction, covering the walls, dropping from the ceiling. He wailed and cursed and stomped and smashed but there was no stopping them. A red centipede slithered up his pant leg and he was sure that this was the moment his mind would finally break, shatter like a piece of fine crystal.

He swatted at his body. Felt them pouring over him, becoming a second skin, trying to pry open his eyelids or wriggle into his nostrils or burrow down his throat. Choking and sputtering he fell to the floor...

And just like that, they were gone. He tried to catch his breath, scanning the room but there was no sign of them. He looked down at his ripped clothes, red and bruised skin. Bruised from his own thrashing. Had any of it been real? Something flitted through his mind; a fragment of memory. Something about confronting fear. There was more meaning attached to it but it was gone, beyond his grasp. Later, he told himself. He could remember later. He was so tired...

Tommy crawled back into bed and fell asleep.

He dreamed of fire.

Flames, hypnotic and destructive. The flames were connected to a memory.

The church. Now he remembered: in return for Dartmoor protesting his brother's funeral, Tommy had set the church on fire. It hadn't burned to the ground; only one wall and part of the roof had been consumed before the firefighters arrived and extinguished the blaze. There had been an investigation, and at the convenience store, security camera footage of Tommy purchasing cans of gasoline. The investigators had questioned him, but the evidence hadn't been enough to arrest him. It was a good thing; he had just turned eighteen and he would have been tried as an adult.

He hadn't gone to jail. But the church knew. One night when they had shown up in the front yard with torches, singing hymns of God's Wrath Dad had chased them away with a shotgun.

And then… what happened then?

Outside, he heard the train whistle. Midnight. Midnight…

Dad had disappeared sometime around midnight. The memories flooded in now… Dad had been on his way to a security job at the junkyard. They found his car at the side of the road at 12:30, the engine still hot. Weeks passed and the police said they had no leads so Tommy had gone to… "the shop."

Over the tracks and under the bridge. UNCANNY was its name. He had only been inside a few times, but he had heard stories. About the old man and the secret room down in the basement, where a person could cast a certain kind of magic, for the right price. Dark magic. The kind that could even up a score or settle a feud. He had gone, and he hadn't needed to say more than two words to the old man. The man had disappeared behind a black curtain and when he came back he offered Tommy the book: RITES, RITUALS AND INCANTATIONS.

Back in the here and now, out in the hall, the sound of chains dragging on the floor. It was coming for him again.

He remembered the basement, where the old man had taken him.

The chains, coming closer.

There had been strange symbols on the floor. Candles. Incense.

Beneath the door to room C6, smoke poured in. A host of insects swarmed amid the mist, across the floor and up the walls.

The man at Uncanny had guided him through the ritual. The summoning. But in order to prove worthy...

He had said Tommy must face his fears. He had brought out a basket. In it had been cockroaches and beetles and spiders. Tommy fought his terror, plunged his hand in; passed the test. The summoning had begun. But the church... they knew. Somehow Dartmoor knew. They had stormed into the basement before the ritual could be completed.

The door to room C6 unlocked and swung open. Fog billowed around a tall, robed, hooded figure as it glided in, dragging rusted chains behind it. The chains hung over its shoulders, looped around its body and left arm, attached to a wooden handle with a curved crescent-moon blade at the end. From its right hand hung a censer. Incense poured from holes in its silver top.

Tommy gazed into the coals that served as eyes in the blackness of the thing's hood.

He remembered. This... was what he had summoned. What he created. Crafted from both imagination and experience. The censer came from his early years in Catholic school, where the priests used them in religious ceremonies. The bladed weapon, a kusarigama, was from his childhood fascination with Japanese history. The robe and hood represented the grim reaper. He had imagined this thing long ago, as a child. But not the bugs. They swarmed all about the visitor, disappearing into and emerging from ragged holes in the cloth, skittering and scuttling over parchment-dry skin. Tommy realized now that the insects represented the fear he conquered.

He had imagined this thing, drawn pictures of it. He had named it the Vindicator. An avenging angel.

That night in the basement of Uncanny, when the church interrupted the ritual Tommy had lost a part of himself, and with it he had lost his mind. But now... now his creation had returned.

The Vindicator held out a skeleton-hand and spread its talon-tipped fingers. Its voice was dry leaves on headstones. "Join me," it said. "Our task remains unfinished."

Tommy reached out and grasped the hand.

The following day, when orderlies asked the other patients what happened to Tommy, each of them swore that the only thing they heard that night was the sound of chains dragging on the tile floor.

The Regrettable Return of John Wiermore

The Regrettable Return of John Wiermore *is a love letter to horror. Although there are Lovecraftian elements to it, it is specifically a love letter to Stephen King. The cosmic horror experienced in this story is not fancy. Its characters are blue collar and the emotions they feel are as real as those that you and I feel. People are often put into circumstances beyond their control. Allowing fictional characters to react like real people if they stared nightmarish horror in the face is quintessential Stephen King.*

The Kitchen

John Wiermore emerged from the mist like a befuddled, silhouetted phantom, the kind that wore a handlebar mustache and a threadbare flannel jacket. Hannah hadn't noticed John standing confused and lost-looking at the end of their long driveway, one foot kicked out almost comically from an ankle injury received during his brief stint in the US Army. It wasn't just the night fog or the way his silhouette was backlit and made bleary by the glittering ice crystals and swarming lights behind him. Mostly it was because she was keeping an eye on the roiling pasta water on the stove and dicing the living shit out of an onion like it was therapy.

A high-pitched noise was drilling into Hannah's skull that she had at first thought was her tinnitus acting up. As she wiped tears from her eyes with the back of her hand and tossed the culprit onions into a hot frying pan, she slowly began to assume that a neighbor's alarm was going off or a powerline was acting up.

"Hon, do you hear that sound? It's driving me crazy," Hannah called out from the kitchen before remembering her husband was picking up Olivia from volleyball practice while she made dinner.

Hannah swore under hear breath and turned to grab a zucchini to dice up for the red sauce when the pitch of the maddening noise spiked, high enough to physically hurt the middle aged woman's ears. She practically threw the carving knife she used to chop most anything while she cooked into the sink and protectively cupped her ears. She stood there, staring down into the porcelain sink waiting for the pain to subside, wondering if she was perhaps having a stroke, just as a sound like fingernails on a chalkboard clawed through her mind and down her spine, pulling her nerve endings out by the root in the process. She could hear as much as feel the pounding of her heart wub-wubbing in her chest and ears. The pounding was so loud and painful, she was certain she really was having a stroke.

Hannah stood there in front of the sink for what to her seemed like a lifetime, gripping the lip of the counter in front of her as if her sanity depended on it, jaw clenched so tightly she was bound to shatter a crown or two. Slowly, the sounds and sensations faded, leaving her feeling ill and clammy in a way Hannah associated with motion sickness. She took a deep breath and tossed cold tap water on her face.

A flash of light outside the kitchen window caught Hannah's eye.

"Thank God my babies are home," Hannah said in a low voice. She was shivering as if a body flu had just struck her. Whatever she just went through, whatever the cause, had been a meat grinder.

Except her babies weren't pulling up in the driveway. It took Hannah a few blinks to realize that a man was standing at the end of her driveway, and that that man wearing his signature blue flannel, baseball cap, and one foot kicked out at an odd angle was also her husband. A different husband. A husband who had gotten fat over time. A husband who had been missing and presumed dead for just over ten years.

"Fuck, maybe I am having a stroke."

The Shed House

John sat in a chair too small for his 6'4", 275-lbs body. The dimly lit shed house sitting in the backyard of what should have been his home felt like a dollhouse to a man of his build. Although it had been his home when he left for work that morning, it clearly no longer was.

He felt like he had walked out of the fog into a world that was no longer his own. He had taken his normal walk back from his furniture factory along the river expecting to find Hannah and Olivia waiting at the dinner table for Wednesday Night Spaghetti Night. It was a family tradition. Instead, he had stepped out of the hoary fog coming off River Walk Lane only to stop dead in his tracks. The house sitting in front of him on property that had been in his family for three generations wasn't his home. After the strange walk he had just endured, he at first assumed he had gotten turned around and was in front of someone else's home. But he recognized the property and the house number was definitely his.

Even after the strange humming and screeching ceased ripping his brain apart and the photophobia-like light show swarming about him had faded, all he could do was stare dumbly at the house that should have been his home.

Naturally, he thought he was losing his mind. Even as Hannah raced out the front door to him, hysterically calling his name over and over, all he could do was look in confusion at the strange world around him. Strange, but familiar. It wasn't the things that were completely different that made him sick to his stomach and feel like his brain had been blended inside his own skull. It was the things that were the same but somehow not the same that threatened to put him over the edge. Even his wife seemed different. More energetic and healthier. Full of a vitality he had not seen in her for close to more than ten years. Even the pretty brunette hair he had fallen in love with in junior high seemed healthier and prettier than it had in years.

He couldn't make out Hannah's frantic words. She was scared and every bit as bewildered as he was. Slowly, he realized she was leading him into their backyard to the prefab Costco shed house that he in no way ever purchased in his entire life and certainly never had delivered to his property.

It was warm and homey. Dimly lit. Hannah had flipped on a bright overhead light while sheep dogging him into the 12 x 24 accommodation, but the light hurt John's eyes so badly he started flailing out like an overstimulated autistic kid. Hannah switched to a dim table lamp and ushered John to the chair he now sat in.

She had always been good at sheep dogging him around and calming him when he was having social-anxiety issues. It was cozy and had Hannah's taste for home decor written all over it. The kitchen and bathroom were tiny, but that didn't stop Hannah from shoving an over-sized fridge into the place. The smaller kitchen freed up square footage for a sizable living room with a couch and several comfortable chairs. From the uncomfortable chair John sat in at a small table beside the window, he could see that this shed was for entertaining guests and drinking late into the night.

If someone got too drunk, they could climb up to the tiny loft in the back of the shed above the bathroom and slip into a twin bed.

John was certain the couch was a pull out and there was at least one air mattress tucked away in a cabinet somewhere. That was just how Hannah Wiermore operated.

John cracked the window as he lit a fresh cigarette with the butt of the one he had just finished. The butts were piling up in a Mason jar lid he had found in a kitchen drawer. The shed was filling with the smoke. Hannah never smoked and hated the habit John brought back from the Army with him. From the window, he could see his darkened backyard and the house that should have been the family home he had inherited from his dad. The yard looked pretty much as it should, with the exception of the shed house he was chain smoking in and the fire pit flanked by Adirondack deck chairs just off the tiny porch. From there he could see the big window in the back of the house where the family room was. He could make out figures moving behind the drawn blinds and occasionally peering out at him but couldn't tell who they were.

John never felt entirely comfortable or that he belonged anywhere he was, not even in his own home, but never had he felt like an intruder before. Never had he felt like people were scared of him, let alone his own family. He'd be angry and charge right in his own back door and demand to know why he was being treated like a leper if it wasn't for how queasy and jittery he felt after the god-awful walk he had taken along the river. John smashed out his cigarette into the Mason jar lid. Hannah never allowed ashtrays in the house, but she collected Mason jars and an entire host of mismatched lids like a fiend.

He needed a drink and knew a variety of cold beers awaited in the fridge. He found a bottle of some bullshit microbrew before spotting a fifth of Patron sitting on the counter.

"Fuck it," John said with a shrug of broad but slouching shoulders as he grabbed up the bottle. He didn't bother looking for a shot glass as he made his way back to the chair with both bottles.

The Guest

John was taken aback when Mathew Cox let himself into the shed house without knocking. John hadn't seen Mathew in years. He had no idea why the well-groomed man would just let himself in, let alone why he had a fifth of Jack in one hand. Mathew's face grew visibly repulsed as he stepped into the shed only to be blasted by the smoke and whatever BO John was currently stewing in after a long day of working with his hands at the shop.

"Jesus, John," Mathew said, practically gagging, "open a fucking window."

"It is," John replied, distantly, as he adjusted his baseball cap on his head.

Mathew considered the situation, then elected to leave the front door open to air the place out. He sat down across from his hulking old friend, slamming the bottle of Jack down onto the table with showmanship.

"Let's drink," the smaller man pronounced, a specter of his salesman grin hunting about, judging to see if it was safe to come out and play with the brooding man across from him.

John took a deep drag of his cigarette and let the smoke do whatever the fuck it wanted as he spoke: "Beat you to it," he said in a low, weary voice.

Mathew cocked both eyebrows and nodded his head as he glanced at the table between them. Flanking the pile of butts building up in the Mason jar lid were a few empty bottles of the microbrew and a severely diminished bottle of Patron.

"Wow, yeah, you have," Mathew concluded. "I hope you don't mind if I join you."

John didn't care enough to scoff. He was well on his way to drinking his problems gone. He had grown tired of Mathew's smug attitude years ago, long before they finally parted ways as business partners.

Mathew saw he was getting nowhere with his old friend, so crossed the shed to the kitchen to find a couple of clean tumblers. He filled them both from the ice cube dispenser on the front of the fridge before trying another attempt.

"Do you like the beer?" Mathew asked. "It's from a company I'm part owner of."

"It's fine for fag beer," John replied, not bothering to do anything besides stare absently out the window of what should have been his backyard as his cigarette smoldered in his stained, chubby fingers.

Mathew sighed. That was the John Wiermore he remembered. He knew his old friend enough to appreciate when it was pointless to try small talk on him. He crossed back to the table and poured Jack for them both. As he sat, he demonstrably slid the tumbler to John.

"Okay, John. Let's skip the chit chatting part and get right to it."

Mathew leveled knowing eyes at a man who was once a dear friend, a business partner. John couldn't be bothered to acknowledge that he even heard the man.

Ice clinked as Mathew drank his drink down in one gulp. He poured himself another before stating as calm and matter-of-factly as one could, "John, how the fuck are you alive and sitting in my backyard?"

The Conversation

John flinched at the question, but otherwise continued to slowly pull from his cigarette and stare in the general direction of the family room of the house that was no longer his home. He blew a thick plume of smoke out the window before speaking.

"You've always been a hyper-active, overly-entitled little fucker, but please go on and explain to me how my backyard belongs to you."

"Because, John, you've been dead for ten years. Well, technically, you've been missing and are presumed dead. No one ever found your body."

John turned to level his big, watery eyes on his obnoxiously-handsome old friend. At one time, John was handsome himself. In a different way than Mathew, but he was good enough to get Hannah Millhouse when she was still in her prime. Now, in the dark room, chubby cheeks more like jowls, double chin, pouty lips, crow's feet, stained teeth, reeking from a day of working in a factory... Well, John looked like the kind of trash human that lived in a van down by the river. Those big dumb cow eyes couldn't intimidate a school kid now. But Mathew knew John wasn't a total idiot. Mathew knew John had the strength of a man John's size and the temper to use it if push came to shove. Mathew was intimidated by John.

Physically at least.

John rolled his shoulders around as if in great discomfort and slid a hand into his lap. Mathew didn't like that at all. He wanted to see both John's hands at all times. John rubbed at his neck with one hand, cigarette pinched between fingers. To Mathew, it looked like the man was about to crawl out of his own fat skin suit.

"I'm sitting right here, Matt," the bigger man finally said, unable to properly focus his eyes on his old friend. "What the fuck do you mean I've been missing? I haven't so much as missed a single day of work in fifteen years."

Mathew's right hand slipped into his own lap as he brought his drink to his lips with the other. At the sound of the clinking ice cubes, he nearly jumped up and pulled the .357 Magnum out from where he was hiding it in the folds of his baggy sweater. John might not know why he should be dead, but Mathew sure the fuck did.

"How is that possible when I killed you myself ten years?"

Mathew watched John's body language closely. His old business partner recoiled a little at his words. Not in shock. Like the truth hurt. John rubbed at the back of his neck and cupped the back of his skull as if something inside of him was burrowing its way out. John had to what Mathew looked like a neck spasm, and he watched as the entire side of John's neck seemed to bulge and undulate. It was probably just a trick of the light, but whoever this John was he wasn't a healthy man.

John slowly opened his mouth, presumably to speak, but to Mathew it looked like his jaw was about to unhinge so the bigger man could swallow him up whole. John worked his jaw, confused as to why his words wouldn't come.

"I'm. Sitting. Right. Here," the hulking man said, finding his words. "And you are telling me this is your home? Okay, then why is Hannah still living here? Why can I see her and my baby girl peeking out at me from the family room window like I'm some kind of rogue bear they just called the game commission on?"

"Have a drink, John," Mathew instructed, indicating John's tumbler of Jack and melting ice.

John glanced at it and tossed his cigarette into it before reaching for the Patron bottle.

Mathew gripped the handle of the magnum in his lap, wishing that he could see what John's hand was doing in his own lap. That fat bastard could be so damn stubborn.

"Fine. I'm tired of trying this nice. Here's the thing, John: You're dead. I know you're dead because I killed you myself ten years ago in that shitty shop we used to own together. One late night, I shoved you into a lathe when you were turning bed posts or some shit. Grinded you up like fucking chipped ham. Your blood and guts splattered all over me."

Mathew brought his tumbler to his mouth, his hands shaking so badly the ice tinkled the entire way to his mouth. But at least he finally got John's fat ass attention.

"Sounds kinda sloppy," John replied, incredulous.

"It was, but I planned for it. I had scrubs I stole from my brother a few months earlier. He was just finishing med school back then, and I had been planning to kill you for a long, long time. Long before you fucked up the Aston Furnishings deal. Missing those deadlines and having that half-million purchase order cancelled on us was reason enough to shove you into a fucking lathe, but by then it was just one more God damn reason."

"How did you dispose of my body?" John asked, actually smirking, until a rippling spasm raced up and down the arm he kept partially concealed in his lap so violent Mathew could actually see it. The pain of it robbed the smirk from John's fat, pale face. Mathew wasn't sure how John could look more disgusting and stupid than he normally did, but he pulled it off with all the grimacing and spasming he was doing.

"Simple. Remember that powder we kept by the gallon to clean saw blades? You mix it with water and it became acid?"

John nodded as he lit his last cigarette clumsily with one hand.

"Yeah, well, I sawed your fat ass up with a skill saw and shoved you into drums filled with acid. I sealed those up along with the scrubs and then I torched the fucking shit hole furniture shop we were wasting our lives in."

"Did you ever think of just asking to buy me out?" John asked. Something approximating levity filled his voice, and he began to chuckle. He wasn't sure, under the circumstances, how he could find his sense of humor. But considering he had just walked home after a twelve hour day at the furniture shop with nothing on his mind other than to enjoy Wednesday Night Spaghetti Night with his family just to come home to this? He should have been cackling like a lunatic.

John's chuckle was quickly replaced by a wet cough. Mathew watched more in horror than disgust as John seemed to be gagging, mouth working stupidly as phlegm or some other viscous fluid worked its way out of his mouth and down his knobby chin.

The sight nearly made Mathew throw up, but he decided to keep forging forward. He had every intention of goading his old friend into a fight so he could gun him down fair and square on his own property.

"Buying you out wasn't good enough. I wanted to completely rebuild. I needed you totally out of the way, and I needed the insurance money to rebuild a proper company on property that your idiot family didn't own."

"How would that even work?" John asked. He eyeballed the Patron bottle as he wiped at the viscous goo on his chin, but whatever was tearing up John's insides made him reconsider consuming more tequila. It was probably a trick of the light, but Mathew thought he saw the thin skin of John's wrist bulge and writhe, like a swarm of baby snakes were making their way up and down his dumb, fat arms. But they were gone as quickly as he saw them. It had to have been his imagination. "Hannah would have inherited everything I owned."

"She did," Mathew said with a telling finality. He stared John dead in the eyes, gripping the pistol in his lap, hoping that the slow-witted fool sitting across from him would finally realize what the fuck was going on.

Realization sank home. The big, brown, watery eyes hardened. Dangerously so.

"How long?"

"Do you mean how long were Hannah Cox—not Wiermore, Cox!—and I fucking each other?"

"Yeah."

"Since high school. Almost the entire time you two were together. Whenever she'd get tired of your fat ass three-pumping her missionary style, she'd come to me for some real fucking."

"Even when I was in the Army? You two…" John's words trailed off. Mathew almost felt sorry for the dumb slob.

"You weren't gone long before you fucked up your foot, but, yeah, we fucked the first night you deployed. It was like a celebration."

"She was pregnant with Olivia, Matt," John practically pleaded. "How could you fuck another man's pregnant wife?"

Mathew nearly fell in on himself, dejected by how stupid his old friend was.

"John, you stupid fuck, have you ever done a single math problem in your entire life? Did you ever think to bust out a calendar and use your fingers to count to nine? Hannah got pregnant three months after you deployed. *Three months!* Do the math, you retarded fucking lumber jack."

The Backyard

Mathew barely had time to realize that a half dozen, serpentine tendrils where lashing out at him from across the table before he fully understood that he was in danger. He brought the .357 up and got off a single shot before it was whiplashed out of his hand by one of the slimy tendrils.

The gunfire immediately deafened him. Even through the ringing in his ears, he could hear John roaring in pain and rage as he rose to his full height, realization that his wife had been cuckolding him for decades with their best friend from high school and that it was the two of them that were the blood parents of his only daughter. Before Mathew could even move, John had tossed the table between them aside with the slithering tendrils that had replaced his left arm. With his human hand, he grabbed up the smaller man by his neck and slammed him against the open door of the shed house.

The air in Mathew's lungs expelled in a single blast. As he wheezed and flailed impotently at the hand around his neck, John continued to smash him over and over against the door. Even in middle age, John was a powerfully built man. But the strength he demonstrated in that moment was preternatural. Mathew couldn't think of anything except survival, but as terrified as he was he couldn't help but notice that the Magnum round he had fired had not missed John. It had blasted a hole square in his chest.

Inky goo was seeping out from the chest wound, but it didn't slow the large man down. Nor did it stop the serpentine tendrils protruding from the left sleeve of his battered flannel from flailing and whipping about. Mathew watched as the life was being beaten out of him as the man he murdered ten years earlier transformed in front of him. Big, dark eyes grew bigger and longer. Inky black. More like monstrous holes in the face of the man he once knew. Like the eyes, his mouth fell open, impossibly large as if his jaw really had come unhinged earlier when he was foolishly goading the man into a physical altercation.

Beneath the milky flesh, the skin bulged and writhed and spasmed and squirmed as if a thousand snakes had moved in and hollowed out what should have been John's flesh and bones. Whatever it was inside John was strong. And fast. So fast.

Barely conscious, Mathew realized he was flying through the air and the bleary, wet ground was coming at him fast. He rolled over, propelled by nothing but adrenaline, to face his attacker and immediately realized he shouldn't have done that.

What was once a man named John Wiermore, ten years older than the man Mathew himself had chopped up and tossed into barrels of hydrochloric acid, now stood a horrific, lumbering horror of a creature that was more serpentine tendrils in a vaguely human flesh suit than a human being.

Mathew had just enough time to realize the ringing in his ears wasn't just in his ears. The air around him was filled with it. The high-pitched noise was punctuated by an odd metallic warbling sound and a sensation that was more physical than audible, not unlike fingers on a chalkboard. The sounds were pulverizing his brain. If this was what Hannah had endured earlier that evening, she was a remarkable woman for being as composed as she had been when he had walked through the front door just a few hours prior.

It had been Hannah, not Mathew, who had speculated that John was a glitch in the matrix, a Mandela Effect or Twinner from a Stephen King novel. Like Mathew, she knew it couldn't actually be

John Wiermore. What Mathew hadn't told John, what he hadn't gotten around to telling him before he started getting the life beat out of him, was that Hannah had been in on the murder plot the entire time. John had been way more valuable dead than alive—and the two lovers had gotten really good at tricking John over the years. They'd been fooling the big dumb bastard long before Hannah found herself pregnant with Mathew's baby.

Mathew and Hannah had spent years making sure the family will and insurance policies where just right to maximize the wealth they would receive upon John's death. They both planned the entire thing down to every last detail. The only snag was when John was deemed missing, instead of dead. It took a lot to correct that oversight—but it didn't stop them from being together. It didn't stop them from building condos over the ruins of the furniture factory and John's incinerated remains. It didn't stop them from starting a new, modern shop in an industrial park that they co-owned or taking the profits and remodeling their home. It didn't stop them from loving each other while raising their daughter together.

Mathew couldn't lift himself off the ground. It felt as if a physical force was pushing down on him, a vibrational frequency so strong as to paralyze him. He heard what he thought was a shotgun blast. He watched as an invisible force hit the side of John's face and tore a thousand tiny holes into what was left of his flesh suit. The nightmarish creature slowly turned its head in the direction of the shotgun fire, but the tendrils lashed out without thought, without hesitation, at its attacker.

Mathew was certain he would vomit any second and drown in that vomit as he used every last ounce of determination he had to turn away from the creature that was once John Wiermore. He wished he hadn't as his entire world was taken from him before his own dying eyes.

The tendrils had lashed out, whipping the shotgun out of Hannah's boney arms and around her thin neck. The tendrils had grown long and thick. Even as Mathew watched as the love of his life, the mother of his daughter, was lifted off the ground they continued to grow. Whatever the creature was that had taken over John's body, it thrived on the madness-inducing sounds pulverizing him and his family.

It was then that Mathew realized Olivia was standing helplessly behind her mother as a single tendril reared back, as if taking aim, before plunging effortlessly through Hannah's chest and out the back side of the thin woman. Blood splattered on Olivia's terrified face a split second after she realized her mother had been murdered by the horror in her backyard and just before the tendril stabbed through the vulnerable meat and veins of her young throat.

Mathew let out an involuntary bellow of anguish that rivaled the one that John made just moments earlier inside the shed house as his dead-eyed wife fell to the ground and his beautiful daughter dropped to her knees, hands at her throat, choking to death on her own blood.

Mathew roared and roared in anguish, but the unearthly sounds oppressing him drowned out his own impotent noise. What a fool he had been. What a stupid, arrogant fool he was for bragging about fucking another man's wife to his face, for revealing he had fathered the beautiful daughter that John had thought was his own, who he had raised as his own. What a stupid, arrogant prick he had been for thinking he could murder another man, steal his entire life, then brag about it to his face.

Mathew would never learn how another John Wiermore—a John Wiermore from a world where the two had simply parted ways as business partners and moved on with their lives—appeared on his driveway one night, ten years after dissolving the man's body in acid. But it had happened. And the price for John Wiermore's return was regrettable.

An Excerpt from
The Great Yag

Part II of the Doom Bunny Cycle

> *"The world was full of monsters, and they were allowed to bite the innocent and the unwary."*
>
> –Stephen King, *Cujo*

That's why I was back at Old School Tattoo and Piercing. I wanted more wards and sigils to protect me. The mental clarity and insanity prevention ward was functioning as advertised, but sooner or later the cultists were going to get tired of merely making me feel uncomfortable. They were going to come after me soon. I had asked the squirrely tattoo artist—Tanner was his name for some reason—for a ward that would help make me invisible and harder to track. There was nothing I could do about the cultists knowing where I lived, but I wanted to be able to Uber with a little piece of mind.

It was taking me a while to process Tanner's reply.

"I'm not sure I'm following you," I finally said behind my black N95. It was hot under the mask and I was beginning to break out into a thin sheen of sweat. I hated wearing the damn thing, but I hated the idea of dying alone from COVID with a tube shoved down my throat in an isolation ward even more.

"I can't give that to just anyone. You'll have to do something to earn it," he repeated, slower than the first time.

"So I can't just hand you cash in return for a service that you then render?" I asked, not bothering to hide my white man displeasure.

"Accurate," Tanner replied.

I shook my head and forced myself to not get annoyed by the greasy kid. I needed him more than he needed me, regardless of how punchable his smarmy face was. Besides, how bad could a guy be if he had a life-size Boba Fett statue in the front window of his shop?

"Okay, let me show you something. Maybe we can barter," I reasoned as I pulled folded-up parchment from the cargo pocket of my shorts.

Tanner's eyes lit up as I unfolded the parchment and laid it out on the counter.

"What the actual fuck, dude?" was his reply.

"You tell me. I found it posted on my front door. No idea who left it. Presumably the same person left this chalk drawing as well," I informed Tanner, showing him the pic I had saved on my phone.

I couldn't tell if the twitchy little guy was terrified or thrilled by what I had shared with him. He kept glancing from the symbols to the street outside, as if he were concerned about drawing unwanted attention. It felt like there were eyes burning into my back, but it had felt that way for days now. Like someone or something had set its sights on me. Something powerful.

"You can have it. How many wards can I get in exchange for it?" I asked.

"Put that thing away. I never want to see it again," he demanded. He was really amped up. "Look, I know someone down on the ass end of Cornwall Street who would be interested in that. I was going to ask you to deliver something to her anyway while you were out Ubering," he continued as he looked beneath his counter for something. "I'll give you the invisibility ward and two generic wards of your choosing at my normal hourly rate—*if* you get that parchment the fuck out my shop and hand deliver this to Starship Sarah."

I blinked as Tanner handed me an old cigar box, sun bleached and battered. It was sealed with masking tape. It had been sealed for a long time.

"What is it?" I asked as I took it into my hands and began to study it.

"A box. Don't open it."

"Okay," I replied. His prerogative. "So where on Cornwall is this Starship Sarah person?" I asked, silently bewildered that I found myself living in a world where I would have to ask such a question. "It's a long strip of road."

"Down by the water; near the AA Hall. You'll know her RV when you see it."

I nodded in understanding. Cornwall was a long street that stretched across the entire town from one end to the other. Tanner was referring to the strip of road south of where we were standing, where it nearly ended along the water, parallel to the Burlington Northern rail line. Industrial buildings lined both sides all the way down to where the street ended and Pine abruptly turned off to the left up towards the woods neighborhood by campus. The street ended next to a fairly popular AA hall and a little patch of sandy beach I personally referred to as Meth Beach.

This intersection made up the penis head of Bellingham and Meth Beach was the stinky penis tip. The combined smell of briny sea water, a line of unattended honey buckets, and whatever garbage meth heads left on the beach was not great. I don't know what chlamydia smells like, but this beach probably smelled like it.

Along the way to the penis tip, Cornwall was lined with an assortment of battered RVs, camping vans, and an ever-growing variety of converted vehicles. Most of the dwellers inside those homes were not engaging in van life as a super hip lifestyle choice. They were destitute. Many of them had severe mental health problems and drug habits. Presumably, Spaceship Sarah was among them.

"As long as I don't have to get out of my car at Meth Beach, I'll make sure she gets this," I said, folding the parchment back up.

Tanner smirked at my name for that shitty little section of town before turning his attention to something else behind the counter. I knew when I was being dismissed, so I headed back to the minivan, totally ignoring the filthy, old homeless guy who was standing way too close to my vehicle. It looked like he had just pissed all over my front tire.

I had seen him before around town and limping up and down the back alley behind my house. Shoulder-length gray hair was swooped back to reveal a broad forehead and wild eyes. His hair was more yellow-white. The nicotine effects of chain smoking, most likely. Filthy army fatigues and battered combat boots. He wore an impossibly long scarf wrapped around his neck that dangled in a way that reminded me of one of the Doctor Who incarnations. He dragged one foot behind him that suggested the foot was never going to function correctly again. But the strangest thing was all the facial tattoos. There wasn't a single inch on his face and neck that wasn't tattooed in spirals and over-stylized stars. Primitive and tribal with something of a nautical flair. Even his ears were tattooed.

I avoided eye contact and got the minivan on the road as quickly as I could. I had no idea what meth-head language he had been yelling at me in and didn't care. I had a cigar box to deliver.

Spaceship Sarah's RV wasn't anywhere near the beach and the line of rancid honey buckets. Small favors. Instead, her domicile was pulled up to the curb beside a battery-assembly plant. Her home was a filthy, road-weary 40 footer. It had all the tell-tale signs of significant use. Deep scratches. Dented and dingy paneling. Spider-webbed cracks in many of the windows. Either it had spent a lot of time deep in national parks or on side roads just like Cornwall being used as a tweaker den.

The RV was blocked. One wheel was up on a jack and tarps were propped up around the side door in a way that created an enclosure. More tarps covered the roof from stem to stern, presumably to prevent water from leaking in. The smoking grill and icebox sitting in front of all that led me to believe it had been some time since the RV had moved. I had no idea how it hadn't been towed.

I parked across the street from the RV to study the area while I slipped on nitrile gloves that matched my mask. Other trailers and vans lined the street, but I was certain the RV with the plethora of decorative lights strung up and around it belonged to Spaceship Sarah. In part because of all the chalk symbols scribbled on the street around the RV.

I walked around the front of her home, noting a stack of tickets under the wiper blade and taking in the smell of freshly cooked meat as well as the sound of the vehicle's generator before approaching the side door. Not a great olfactory sensation.

I felt stupid knocking on the tarp, but I wasn't about to trespass.

"Hello?! I have a delivery from Tanner. From Old School?" I shouted as loud as I could through my mask.

Silence. Creepy silence only a creepy silent person could make.

"Hey! If this is Spaceship Sarah's home, I have a package for you. Can I please hand it to you? I'm wearing a mask and gloves," I called out. Louder.

Finally a deep, masculine voice stated, "I don't know a Tanner."

I sighed. Maybe I had the wrong RV. Clearly the mental clarity ward was not helpful when it came to keeping my lack of patience with my fellow man at bay. Maybe Tanner had something for that…

"He knows Sarah. Is she home?" I asked. "I also have something I want to show her. Some symbols on a sheet of paper that someone left on my property. Creepy shit Tanner didn't want anything to do with."

More silence. Different this time. I could feel the contemplation hanging in the air.

"Tanner with the punching face?" the male voice asked.

"Yup," I chuckled. Whoever the guy was, I was going to like him.

"Okay, come on in," the deep voice replied.

I worked my way through the small tarp enclosure and opened the screen door of the RV. It was dark inside and I could now see that most of the windows were covered in blackout paper from the inside. As I stepped up into the RV as an overhead light turned on. I was more than a little surprised to find Doom Bunny, always shirtless, sitting at a cluttered dining nook. He was adjusting a familiar helmet with metal bunny ears onto his head.

"Oh, hey," I said, forcing my eyes to not reveal how surprised I actually was at the sight of him. He had clearly slipped on his helmet after he told me to enter. "So...you are not Starship Sarah."

A muted chuckle emanated from behind the crazy, matte-black helmet. Even with the lights on, the cluttered RV was dimly lit.

"No," came that deep, muffled voice I was all too familiar with.

"That's me," came a female voice from the back of the RV.

A willowy, dark-complected woman with a mess of long black hair strode out of the back bedroom of the camper. She was not what I was expecting at all. Normally, women as young and attractive as Starship Sarah did not live on the side of the road in meth dens—at least not ones with a full set of teeth like Sarah had.

I followed her with my eyes as she strode into the main area of her RV and walked up to a control panel. She didn't bother looking at me while she fiddled with all the knobs and buttons. I couldn't tell what she was doing. To me, the panel made about as much sense as the panel on Darth Vader's chest armor.

She couldn't be bothered to look at me, but I couldn't take my eyes off the lanky, hook-nosed bohemian woman. Her energy filled the interior of the RV. So there I was, holding a cigar box ogling the owner of the RV while she fiddled with knobs and buttons and Doom Bunny stared at me behind the mesh visor of his crudely-fabricated helmet.

"Please, take a seat," the woman said, absently, as she dialed something into the panel and the sound of the diesel generator started to die. "Make yourself at home while I put on tea."

"Yeah, sure," I said as I set the battered cigar box onto the dining table and slid into the padded bench across from Doom Bunny. It felt as surreal to me as it probably does to you. "Good to see you again," I told Doom Bunny as I wiped the clammy sweat from my hands. The mental clarity ward kept the anxiety at bay in my head—but my sympathetic nervous system still acted normally some of the time.

Doom Bunny tried to nod like a normal human, but the huge helmet with the padded shoulders prevented such things.

"What kind of tea do you like?" Sarah asked as she lit the gas range and set the tea kettle onto the flame. "I have everything."

I only knew Earl Grey because I loved Star Trek, so that's what I asked for.

"I don't have that. I'll make you matcha. It's super healthy and will give you a little vroom."

I shrugged.

"So what do you have for me?" Sarah asked, as she turned to lock eyes with me for the first time. I flinched at the sight of them. They weren't wild like she was crazy or anything, but they were very, very intense. Watery brown yet crisp. You didn't go swimming in those eyes, they swam in you. If that doesn't make sense, imagine how I felt staring into them.

"What's in the box?" she asked.

Subscribe to the Nightmare Alley YouTube Channel to continue following *The Doom Bunny Cycle.*

ACKNOWLEDGMENTS

ABOUT THE AUTHOR

Professor Spooky is a figment of the internet's imagination. He is the de facto ringleader of the Nightmare Alley collective of horror writers and deep diver of the dark web. When he's not in hiding from the black ops operatives of the ESD or otherdimensional entities, he's busy scribing the Urban Legends and Creepypasta that seem to find their way into his lap.

ABOUT THE EDITOR

Amanda Faustina is a lover of books, horror, and all things creepy and Gothic. When Amanda isn't devouring horror novels or Creepypasta, she can be found commenting on the Nightmare Alley YouTube channel or editing books like the one you hold in your hands.

ABOUT NIGHTMARE ALLEY

We are Nightmare Alley, a small collective of horror writers dedicated to delivering scary, spooky, and just plain strange stories to fellow horror fans. Urban Legends, Creepypasta, True Crime, and tales of supernatural events are what fuel us. Real or imagined? You be the judge...but we will never reveal our sources. We are merely the humble narrators.

PLEASE JOIN THE NIGHTMARE ALLEY COMMUNITY

Like what you see? Please consider visiting the Nightmare Alley YouTube channel or following us on Facebook. Keep an eye out for our upcoming Patreon campaign. Every click helps bring more terror into the world!

www.ingramcontent.com/pod-product-compliance
Lightning Source LLC
Chambersburg PA
CBHW051925220626
47052CB00003B/573